# More Than I Bargained For

### JESSICA LEIGH JOHNSON

FROST & FAITH
• PUBLICATIONS •

Identifiers: 9798987438022 (trade paper)

9798987438039 (ebook)



Edited by Lora Doncea/Edits by Lora

Cover Design by LaolanArt



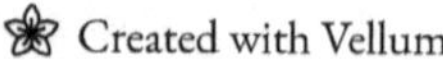 Created with Vellum

*To my fellow "second Thursday of the month" food bank helpers.
This one is for all of you.
And yes, John, I did bring my purse.*

Today must be perfect. A little girl's happiness is at stake. And that little girl won't be happy if she's starving. *Come on, turkey. Cook faster!*

Pacing the kitchen has become my go-to outlet for all my pent-up energy. My older sister and niece are already in the dining room, eagerly awaiting the Thanksgiving feast that I promised them. But things are running a teensy bit behind schedule—okay, maybe a *lot* behind schedule. Dinner was already going to be late to begin with because I promised we wouldn't eat too early. My sister, who recently switched to working nights as a med-surg nurse at the hospital, needed her sleep after a twelve-hour shift. But now it's almost five, and she works again in two hours. With all the prep work, I somehow forgot to serve lunch, so everyone's blood sugar—and patience—is running a little low.

Seriously, though, who knew these overgrown chickens took so long to cook?

When the oven timer dings, I jump to attention. The hour of reckoning is here. Either this turkey is done, fully-cooked, melt-in-your-mouth perfection—or it's still somewhat slimy, bordering on raw, and likely to poison us all with salmonella.

I'm hoping for the former. It *has* been in the oven for five hours, and I'm pretty sure this thing was thoroughly thawed when I stuck it in there, so the odds are in my favor.

Wincing against the heat, I pull the massive bird from the oven, then set the roasting pan on the stovetop. I stand back and gaze in awe at what I've accomplished. On the outside, I have to say it looks pretty good. Golden brown, crispy skin and a heavenly aroma that evokes memories of childhood holidays. Twenty-two pounds was probably a bit ambitious for my first attempt at cooking a turkey, especially for only three people ... but it'll all be worth it when Tamara and Kelsey take their first bites and realize that maybe I *do* know what I'm doing in the kitchen. Plus, with a turkey this size, we'll have leftovers for days.

And days.

Tamara appears at my side, startling me. "Do you need help?" she asks, her tone bordering on panicked. "I'll get the side dishes on the table." She rushes back and forth to carry out the mashed potatoes, dinner rolls, and cranberry sauce.

Once I've finished carving the meat into nice, even slices, I transfer what I can to a platter and carry it into the dining room. Both Tamara and Kelsey are seated, eyes on the turkey.

Kelsey smiles and claps her hands. "I can't wait!"

Grinning at her, I carefully lower the full platter to the center of the table, right between two pumpkin-scented candles, hoping I won't light my sleeves on fire. *Thunk.* The long-stemmed glasses at each table setting tremble, but thankfully none tip over. I need this holiday season to be perfect. For Kelsey.

I sit at the head of our small dining table and see her blue eyes shining—for the first time in a while. A feeling of satisfaction warms my insides. I lean toward her. "So, who wants to say what they're thankful for?"

Kelsey's brow suddenly wrinkles.

"Oh, have you never done this?" I hold out my hands. "Okay then, since this is my first Thanksgiving with you guys—the first of many, I hope—I thought it'd be nice to start with an old family tradition."

Tamara places a gentle hand on my arm. "Anna, I appreciate what you're trying to do, but I work at seven."

I wave off her concern. "We have plenty of time." I clear my throat and focus on Kelsey. "As I was saying ... when your mom and I were younger, your grandparents wouldn't let us eat Thanksgiving dinner until we each said three things we were thankful for."

Tamara cuts in. "And if I remember correctly, you never liked that tradition."

I shoot her a look. "Maybe not, but now that I'm older, I appreciate the ritual. It's good to express our thanks. Don't you agree?"

She stares blankly back at me. "I know it's futile to argue with you, so let's do it."

"Great. I'll go first." I rub my hands together before folding them. "Let's see ... I'm thankful for my new job at the art center because it brought me back home where you both live." I give my sister a knowing wink. "I'm also thankful that you haven't turned my old room into a personal gym so I have somewhere to stay while I'm getting settled. Lastly, I'm thankful that we get to spend the holidays together this year." I turn to my niece. "Okay, Kelsey, tell me three things you're thankful for."

Kelsey's gaze drops to her plate.

Because I've been living out of state for several years, I have to admit I don't know my niece all that well. She was only two when I graduated from college and moved across the country. And even though we've been sharing a house for the past couple of months, she's still shy around me. "Okay, then, I'll let you off easy," I tell her. "How about telling us just one thing you're thankful for."

Kelsey's lower lip trembles. The little girl casts a cautious glance at her mother, then pushes her chair away from the table and bolts from the dining room.

My hand flies to my chest. "Oh, Tamara, I'm so sorry. What was I thinking? How incredibly stupid of me."

"It's okay."

"No, it's not. I can't believe I put her on the spot like that." I'm tempted to bury my face in the steaming bowl of mashed potatoes. Poor Kelsey. What does the little girl have to be thankful for this year? That the father she hasn't seen in six months isn't here on Thanksgiving like he promised he would be? Or that he decided to extend his contract with the pipeline crew and stay in North Dakota for who knows how long? I rake my hands through my messy curls. "I should go talk to her."

Tamara tosses her napkin on the table and stands. "No, I'll go."

Right. I've done enough already. "Please tell her I'm sorry."

Tamara offers a sympathetic smile, then heads down the hall.

Unsure what to do with myself, I rise from the table, lift the enormous turkey platter, and carry it back to the kitchen. I cover it with foil and return it to the oven. From the look I saw on little Kelsey's face, I have a feeling they'll be in her bedroom for a while.

I lean against the counter, my eyes glued to the digital oven clock. Five minutes pass. Then ten. From down the hall I can hear muffled sobs.

*Way to go, Anna.* After spending weeks planning this day, doing everything I can to make it special for Kelsey and Tamara, I've gone and ruined it with a single question. I shake my head and return to the dining room. With a gentle puff, I blow out both candles and cover the basket of rolls with a cloth napkin before sinking into a hard wooden chair.

Why does life have to be so unfair? Tamara and I are no strangers to grief, having lost both our parents in one single, terrible accident during our college years. But as devastating as that experience was, we never had to wonder if our parents loved us. Mom and Dad wouldn't have left if given the choice.

But what about Kelsey? Does she know how loved she is, even if her dad isn't around much to show it?

Footsteps shuffle across the carpeted hallway, and I turn my head to see my sister enter the dining room.

"How'd it go?" I ask.

Tamara shakes her head. "She asked me why her daddy isn't here for Thanksgiving. I'm trying to answer all her questions with honesty, but some things she's too young to know. I feel like I'm always straddling the line between giving too much information and not enough."

"You're in a tough spot," I say. "Kelsey's only five. It can't be easy."

"All the little girls in her kindergarten class talk about their daddies and how they take them snowmobiling or ice fishing. Kelsey can't contribute much to those conversations. She can't even remember what she and Wayne did the last time he visited. He probably played video games while she sat on the floor and watched."

We sit in silence for several minutes. A little while later, I tilt my head toward the hall. "You know what? I haven't heard a sob for a little while. Think it's safe to check on Kelsey?"

Tamara shakes her head. "Let's just give her another minute or two."

"Sure. Okay. The turkey's staying warm in the oven, so we can eat when she comes back to the table. Maybe we can still recover this Thanksgiving dinner."

"Maybe," Tamara says. "But if it's a bust, don't worry. You'll get a chance to redeem yourself a month from now."

"A month? Oh, right. Christmas." I bite my lower lip. "That's one holiday I'd prefer not to tackle on my own."

Tamara laughs. "Don't stress about it. I'll cook the meal if you keep Kelsey entertained."

"Deal. And if there's anything else you need between now and then—we're talking tree decorating, carol singing, Christmas gift shopping—you just let me know. I'm here to help."

Tamara presses her lips together and narrows her eyes. "Do I have your word on that?"

"Um ... yes?" My stomach tightens. Why do I have the feeling I've just committed to something I'm not qualified for? But whatever it is, I'll do it. I'll do anything for Kelsey.

CHAPTER 2

Anna

Once Kelsey calmed down, the three of us managed to have a rather hurried and lukewarm version of a Thanksgiving feast. It was still enjoyable, but not the greeting card holiday I had pictured in my head.

But that's life. It rarely goes according to plan, yet somehow we get through it.

After packing the leftovers in the fridge, I sit on the couch with my feet up on the ottoman. Tamara stands across the living room, dressed in her scrubs, angrily jabbing her finger against her phone screen. My guess is she's texting Wayne, and from the look on her face, he's not responding—or maybe he is, and she doesn't like what he's saying. Either way, I try to mind my own business.

A few moments later, she slams her phone face down on the coffee table, then begins pacing the floor in front of me. I so badly want to bring up the elephant in the room, and seeing how this day couldn't get much worse, I dive right in and tackle the touchy subject. "So ... have you heard from Wayne?"

Tamara huffs. "Only because *I* texted *him*. It's a holiday, Anna, and he hasn't seen Kelsey in months. Even if he can't make it back for a visit, is it really asking too much of him just to call her? She's his daughter." Tamara shakes her head vigorously. "I don't know what to do anymore. I can't keep making excuses for him."

I bite my lip. "I'm so sorry."

Tamara drags both hands down her face. "This is what I get for ignoring all the red flags—and there were more than a few of them, not the least of which being the fact that he didn't believe in marriage." She curls her fingers into quotes on that one. "You know, I almost broke things off in the very beginning, but ... then Kelsey was on the way. I thought maybe becoming a father would spark something inside him, but no. Kelsey was barely three months old, and he was out the door."

"I wish he would realize what a great kid he has." Swinging my legs off the ottoman, I stand and approach my sister, then wrap my arms around her in a tight hug. "You can't blame yourself for Wayne's lack of commitment, and you couldn't have predicted how things would turn out when you first met him. You were twenty years old and grieving. I don't think either of us was capable of making a good decision after losing Mom and Dad." And we both proved it by running straight into the arms of men we shouldn't have trusted.

Tamara sighs. "They would be so disappointed in how my life turned out."

I step back, bracing her shoulders and pinning her with my gaze. "Don't say that. They'd be proud of you for finishing school and becoming a nurse, and they would absolutely love being grandparents."

"They would've been amazing grandparents."

"The best."

She twists the heart-shaped pendant that hangs from her neck. "You and I make quite a pair, don't we? Both terrible judges of character and completely lost without the guidance of our parents."

I laugh, even though the truth of her words is far from comical. "We're doing the best we can, although it sure would be nice to have a good heart-to-heart with Dad every now and then."

"He would've given Wayne *the speech*." She deepens her voice on those last two words. "It would've either sent him running or scared him into submission."

Tamara's absolutely right. Our dad wouldn't have stood for the games Wayne played while dating my sister—his wandering eye, his total lack of commitment. Dad would've insisted that Wayne either marry Tamara or take a hike. Unfortunately, Wayne did take a hike, but only after there was a child in the picture.

I'm a little less sure what Dad would've thought of my ex-fiancé, Brady, who exhibited no red flags whatsoever—at first. He almost seemed too good to be true. But he showed his true colors eventually, when he decided to date someone else while we were trying the long-distance thing. Thankfully, I didn't have a child with the man, so I could walk away from our relationship with only a broken heart. My sister wasn't so lucky. Watching Tamara navigate single parenthood while trying to shelter her five-year-old daughter from some of the uglier aspects of life has been almost unbearable, and I can't imagine what it would have done to our parents.

Tamara wipes a tear from her cheek, then clears her throat. "Anyway, I know I've said it before, but thanks for being willing to move back home. I couldn't have taken the night shift without someone here to stay with Kelsey. It won't be forever, I promise. I know it was a huge imposition for you, not to mention a pay cut."

With a wave of my hand, I dismiss her concern. "Don't be silly. There was nothing left for me in Seattle other than my job." A job I never would've taken if Brady hadn't made it sound like *such* an adventure. "Besides, you know I would do anything for you guys."

"I do, but even so, a day shift should be opening up in a couple of months, and I really hope to be considered for it. I think I have a good chance. Then I'll work mostly while Kelsey's at school, and you can have your freedom back."

I roll my eyes. "Freedom to do what? It's not like I have a life outside of work."

The corners of Tamara's eyes crinkle when she smiles. "You know, there are ways to go about changing that. You could let me set you up on a date. I know a few single doctors who might be interested."

"No, thank you!" I say as I wrap my arm around her shoulder. "It's just you, me, and Kelsey against the world." I pump my fist into the air like a heavyweight champion boxer, and as I do, my sights land on the clock on the wall. It's six forty-five. "Don't you have to get going?"

She heaves a breath. "I do. But there's one more thing I really need from you, and I wouldn't ask except for the fact that I can't make it happen on my own."

"What is it?"

Tamara nods toward the open hall closet, where Kelsey's coat, backpack, and winter boots are piled in a heap on the floor. "Yesterday after school, I was going through Kelsey's school things, and I found her November journal. The teacher has the students draw a picture each day of the month, and beneath the picture they write what they've drawn. Of course kindergarteners can only spell a few words, but they do their best to sound out what they don't know. Tuesday's journal entry was about turkeys, but for Wednesday's page, the topic was 'What I Want for Christmas.'"

"And what does Kelsey want?"

"According to the journal, she wants a TeddyTab."

"A what?"

"You haven't heard? It's a teddy bear and a smart tablet with an indestructible seven-inch screen all rolled into one. They're the biggest toy this season. I had no idea Kelsey wanted one until I saw her journal."

"So are you going to get her one?"

Tamara scoffs. "It's not that simple. For starters, they're impossible to find. But even if you can find one, they're $250."

"Are you insane?" I clamp my hand over my mouth, then let it slide down to my chin. "I mean, that's a little steep for a child's toy."

"Exactly." Tamara nods. "But here's where I could use your help. Normally, a gift like that would be way out of my price range, but I did see in the Black Friday flyer that Big Dealz is getting a limited quantity of TeddyTabs, and they're fifty dollars off before eight a.m. It's a doorbuster deal."

"That's still two hundred dollars," I say.

"I know, and that's still a lot, but I thought maybe if we both went in on it, it wouldn't be so bad." She holds my gaze. "So what do you think? Big Dealz isn't open tonight, only tomorrow morning. You could take a chance. Get up early, stand in line, freeze to death for a super-expensive toy. I'd go myself, but I don't get off until seven a.m., and by then they'll probably be gone."

"But what about Kelsey? She'll still be in bed. And even if I woke her up, I can't exactly bring her with me if I'm shopping for her Christmas gift."

Tamara waves a hand through the air. "I've already texted Mrs. Atkins down the road. She'll be watching Kelsey tomorrow while we're at work since there's no school. I asked if she'd mind coming a little earlier…"

"How much earlier?"

"Around five fifteen."

I can feel my eyes bug out. "Five fifteen in the morning? That woman is a saint."

"She says she's an early riser," Tamara says with a shrug. "Anyway, the store opens at six, and you'll need to get in line well before that." Her eyes zero in on mine. "So do you think you could go? If you find a TeddyTab, we'll split the cost."

Two hundred bucks is a tad steep for a child's Christmas gift. But Tamara *really* wants me to do this for her. "Are you sure this is what Kelsey wants?"

"If it's not, she wouldn't have written it in her journal. Besides, we can always return the bear if we find a better gift idea, but we may not have another chance to buy one after tomorrow."

Hmm. Because of my bright idea to "share what we're thankful for," this year's Thanksgiving will probably go down as an epic fail, but Christmas is only a month away. I will do anything to make it the best one Kelsey has ever had. I realize that what she really wants for Christmas is to have her daddy home, but since I can't just go out to North Dakota and drag Wayne home by his bootlaces, Kelsey will have to settle for the next best thing—a TeddyTab. Is it too much to hope a toy could make a little girl happy, at least for a while?

# CHAPTER 3

# Daniel

I pull the flowery quilt over Madison, tucking her in tightly so she won't fidget. After brushing her bangs away from her eyes, I tap the tip of her nose with my finger. "Today was fun, don't you think?"

My daughter pauses, her eyes much too serious for a six-year-old. "I guess."

"You guess? Come on, you love Thanksgiving. All the good food, the pumpkin pie, playing UNO with Uncle Kurt ..."

She pulls her quilt up to her chin. "I wish Mommy was here."

I sigh. "I know, sweetie. I miss her too. Especially around the holidays."

As much as I love the fact that Madison still talks about her mommy, I can't help but wonder if Madison truly remembers her or if she only remembers the idea of her and the things I tell her. She was only four when Leah passed away, and it's been just shy of two years. How far back can kids remember things?

I lower myself to Madison's bed and nudge her over with my hip, making more room to fit beside her. "Your mom loved decorating the house and baking cookies, and she always had Christmas music playing. I used to get tired of it, but now I miss it."

"You could play Christmas music."

"I will. Just not until tomorrow. Mommy's rule was no Christmas until after Thanksgiving. No Christmas music, no Christmas tree—"

Her eyes light up. "Can we get a Christmas tree? And put presents under it?"

I chuckle at my daughter's enthusiasm. "Sure, we'll get a tree." Of course, there won't be any presents beneath that tree if I don't figure out what to buy. I gently brush my hand against Madison's cheek. "Hey, speaking of presents, what do you want for Christmas?"

Without a word, she rolls onto her side, away from me.

I nudge her shoulder. "Hey, sweet pea, what's wrong? Aren't you gonna tell me what you want this year?"

She shakes her head.

Huh. Apparently, she's not in a helpful mood right now. But that's understandable, given the long day we've had. Maybe tomorrow I'll have her make a Christmas list, give me a few ideas so I'm not way off base with my gift buying this year.

If my wife were still here, she wouldn't even need a list. Leah always knew the perfect gifts to buy for everyone. It was like a sixth sense. Women's intuition. I, on the other hand, need specific instructions. Go to *this* store. Buy *this* toy.

I tuck a wisp of brown hair behind Madison's ear. "Listen, honey, I know you miss Mommy. I miss her too. Every day. And I know she probably wishes she could spend Christmas with you. But for some reason, God decided it was time for Mommy to live in heaven."

She rolls onto her back once more. "Why would he do that?"

I release a long, slow breath. "I don't know." And believe me, I've spent almost two years trying to come to terms with it. "But I do know that Mommy's in the most amazing place we could ever imagine, and that she's so happy there. I also believe she wants us to be happy too, especially at Christmastime."

My little girl's lip quivers as she nods. "Okay." And my heart breaks a little more.

I give her earlobe a little tug. "I have an idea. Why don't you give me one hint about what you'd like for Christmas."

"I don't need to tell you, Daddy. Santa knows what I want."

"I see." I slide off the bed and stand, letting the topic rest for tonight. Christmas is still a month away. I have plenty of time. "You just get some sleep now, and we'll talk about presents later."

"Okay. Goodnight, Daddy."

"Goodnight." I turn off the bedroom light and slip through the doorway into the hall, pulling the door closed behind me. As I make my way downstairs, I can't help but feel defeated. When did the holidays get so complicated? When I was young, I was satisfied to wake up on Christmas morning and find a reel wound with fishing line and some tackle under the tree. But I'm a guy. What does my six-year-old daughter want? A doll? Princess dress-up clothes?

When my feet reach the plush living room carpet, my brother-in-law, who is still sitting on my couch watching football, turns to me with a hopeful expression. "Hey, do you have any more of that whipped cream in a can? My pie's a little dry."

I groan and shake my head. "You know where the refrigerator is."

His brow furrows. "What's eating you? The hardest part of the day is over. Now you can relax."

I fall back into my recliner and pull the handle, releasing the leg rest. "I don't know what to get Madison for Christmas."

Kurt gives me a slow, drawn-out nod. "Ah. Well, thankfully, you have plenty of time to figure it out."

I crack open a warm can of cola that's been sitting out all evening. Light brown foam bubbles out of the small opening, but I drink it down before it spills over the edge and onto my fingers.

Kurt leans forward. "You know what? Now that you mention it, a commercial came on while we were watching the parade this morning."

"You mean while I was cooking and mentioned several times that I could use some help?"

"Hey, I was helping. I was keeping your kid out of the kitchen."

"Thanks so much."

"Anyway, a commercial came on for this bear. It was called a ... Tablet Teddy or something."

"A TeddyTab?" I only know this because I've seen the commercial myself. It's on every hour of every day, and it's only going to get worse as Christmas approaches. I'm pretty sure the catchy little jingle is permanently burned into my prefrontal cortex.

Kurt pokes his finger into the air. "Yeah, that's it. A Teddy-Tab. I'm telling you, Madison wants one. She literally jumped in the air and did one of those cheerleading-slash-karate kicks when it came on TV."

"Really? That's what she wants?" I shift in my seat. "Aren't they kind of pricey?"

Kurt shrugs. "Beats me. But I do remember seeing an ad for a sale tomorrow morning. Limited quantity, fifty bucks off ... if only I could remember where."

I swipe the Black Friday flyers from the end table, and right there on the top of the stack is the Big Dealz ad, boasting a sale on the prized toy. "Two hundred bucks? That's the *sale* price?"

"I didn't say it made sense," Kurt says. "It's just what she wants. You don't have to get it."

No, I don't. But I want my daughter to be pleased when she opens her presents on Christmas morning. And I just found out exactly what she wants—a miracle in itself. So I'll go to that store at the crack of dawn and brave the crowds, hoping to get my hands on one of those crazy-expensive bears.

"Hey, Kurt. What do you think about staying over? I might run to the store in the morning, and I need someone to be here with Madison. I'll be back before you're even awake. You can have the couch."

"I love this couch." He rubs the plush upholstery with his palm.

"I know you do." It doesn't take much to make Kurt happy—just a dark room, a few soft pillows, and a blanket. He's just like a baby.

Feeling a little less panicked about the holidays, I lay back as far as my recliner will go and close my eyes. But not long after, doubts begin to surface. Should I be spending two hundred dollars on one toy, hoping it'll make my grieving daughter happy? Material things don't have that kind of power. Only God has the power to truly mend broken hearts. So what am I even doing, trying to buy her happiness?

I sigh, then send up a silent prayer. *Dear Lord, I am way out of my element here. My daughter needs her mom, but all she has is me. I could really use some guidance so I don't botch Christmas for the second year in a row.*

At times like this, I feel Leah's absence like a hollow ache in my soul. I drag a hand down my face.

Maybe it would be easier if I just tell Madison the truth about Santa.

# CHAPTER 4

# *Anna*

I arrive at Big Dealz at five thirty Friday morning, still half asleep and desperate for caffeine. The instant I step out of my car, a blast of wind hits me square in the face. I pull my knit hat over my ears and walk toward the store's entrance. My breath hitches when I catch sight of the line that begins at the doors, stretches the entire length of the building, and then wraps around the far south wall. If every person standing in line is here for a TeddyTab, I will never get one.

This was a bad idea. Too bad Tamara practically did a backflip when I told her I'd stand in line to get Kelsey the ultra-expensive bear slash tablet.

Sighing, I dig through my purse in search of my phone. Maybe I should call Tamara and tell her it's too late. The line is too long. That will be easier than fighting the mob gathering outside the storefront. But just as the thought crosses my mind, an image of Kelsey replaces it. Sweet Kelsey, tearing the wrapping paper off the techy bear toy on Christmas morning with a huge smile on her all-too-often downcast face.

I pick up the pace. This might be a waste of time, but I won't know unless I try. Hopefully the other shoppers are all here to score the latest 4K HDR gaming console.

I pull my coat tight around myself as I jog past the die-hard shoppers, huddled together and shivering, their breaths coming out in puffs of white. I turn the corner in search of the end of the line when my heel slides on a patch of ice. Arms flailing in the air, I try to stay upright, but it's no use. I fall back and land flat on my hind end in the middle of the cold, damp parking lot, ten feet from a sea of onlookers who have nothing better to do than stare at me.

Despite the frigid temperature, heat infuses my cheeks. How could I have been so clumsy?

*Just get up and pretend like nothing happened.*

I place my bare hands on the ground for support, and a hundred tiny needles pierce my fingertips. I look down to see that I've just placed my right hand in a puddle of icy slush.

Of course.

As I shake the water droplets from my fingers, two brown work boots stop in front of me. A large, leather-clad hand reaches down from above. Without thinking, I grab hold of the hand and allow myself to be pulled up. My gaze travels the length of a pair of dark blue jeans, which lead to a red plaid flannel shirt and a navy vest. When I'm back on my feet again, my eyes lock with those of my knight in shining armor—eyes so creamy brown, I find myself in serious need of a caramel macchiato.

"Are you all right?"

A macchiato with thick caramel syrup drizzled in a zigzag pattern on top of whipped cream, and maybe a few sprinkles of nutmeg and cinnamon ...

"Hello?"

"What?" It's only when his deliciously distracting eyes widen that I realize I've been staring—and my hand is still in his. "Oh, sorry. Yes, I'm all right. Thank you." I pull my hand from his grip and brush it off on the front of my coat. I swallow, seeking moisture for my suddenly dry throat. "I'm more embarrassed than anything. I should've watched where I was walking."

"And worn different shoes." He points to my feet.

I look down at my skimpy dress boots. Who'd have thought I'd need heavy tread for such an occasion? This was supposed to be a shopping trip. "Right. Not the best choice. In my defense, I assumed I'd be doing most of my walking inside the store." I pull my cold hands up into my coat sleeves. "I didn't expect to park this far from the door, either."

The stranger's handsome face breaks into a grin. "You've never gone shopping on Black Friday before, have you?"

"Is it that obvious?"

"Well, if you expected to get a front-row parking spot half an hour before opening, I'd say you're a first-timer. You've got to get here around four if you want that." With a smile and a nod, he turns and begins walking toward the end of the line.

No way am I letting him get away that easily.

I take short, quick steps in order to keep up with his long strides. But this time I'm more careful where I step. "So if you're such an expert on Black Friday, why are you arriving the same time as me?"

He turns to me and grins. "Good question. Let's just say I'd rather sleep in than be the first in line. And I'm no Black Friday expert. I'm actually a rookie, too, but I've heard plenty of horror stories. That's how I knew to come prepared." One at a time, he removes his leather gloves and holds them out to me. "Here. Your fingers must be freezing."

Shivering, I rub my hands together. "No, thank you. I'm fine."

"We'll be in line for at least another thirty minutes." He nods toward the main doors.

My gaze drifts toward the front of the line, now a good hundred yards away. "I'll be okay. Thanks, though."

I follow him in silence until we reach the end of the line. Securing my place behind him, I take advantage of the chance to examine him up close without his knowledge. His neatly combed hair matches the color of his eyes—light brown. He turns his head slightly, and I notice that his angular jawline is dotted with just the right amount of stubble, revealing that while he has a healthy respect for hygiene, he isn't high-maintenance. He's tall and lean, but his plaid shirt sleeves are tight enough around his biceps to suggest he's no stranger to physical labor.

Maybe it's the plaid shirt, but for some reason I can't shake the image of him with his sleeves rolled up, his hands fisted around a long-handled axe, swinging away at a Norway pine.

*For crying out loud, the man's not Paul Bunyan.*

Reluctantly, I drag my gaze away. I shouldn't be gawking at any man's muscles, let alone those belonging to a man I've just met, a veritable stranger. He could be married. I can't tell because he put his gloves back on. Worse, he could be a serial arsonist or a kidnapper. Sometimes an attractive exterior only serves as a cover-up for a rotten soul. The fact that I now live with my sister and niece is proof of that. After witnessing Tamara's heartache up close, not to mention my own, I know better than to open my heart to just anyone. No matter how good-looking he is.

With my arms folded across my chest, I stand on tiptoes to see over the crowd. The doors are still locked, the line unmoving. It could be a while before I progress from this spot, behind this man who smells *oh* so good. What is that musky scent anyway? Some intoxicating mixture of men's care products and ... pine? Maybe he is a lumberjack after all.

I shiver, and not from the cold. So maybe talking to this man won't hurt anything. If nothing else, it will help pass the time. But what should I say?

As if he heard my internal struggle, the handsome stranger turns around to face me. "What is it that brought you out here so early?"

Why didn't I think of that? Simple. To the point. "Just something in the ad. You?"

"Same."

"I see. You're here for one of those gaming consoles?"

He shakes his head. "I'm not much of a gamer. And I'm not shopping for myself. Like I said, I'd rather be sleeping right now. I'm here to buy a gift."

"For ...?" *Please don't say your wife. Please don't say your wife.*

"My daughter."

I wince. That's just as bad. If this guy has a daughter, then there's most likely a woman in his life. And if there isn't, then why isn't there? Maybe this *charming* man is nothing but a carbon copy of my sister's ex, someone who doesn't take his commitments seriously. And that's not something I'm interested in.

I paste on a smile, then turn to face away from him. Time to bow out of the conversation. I don't want to know anything more about this guy that could lead me astray. My fascination with his eyes is bad enough.

I pull my phone from my coat pocket to check the time. Five forty. Time is crawling by. I repocket my phone, then start blowing into my hands to warm them. When a pair of black gloves appears in my periphery, I look up.

"Here," the handsome stranger says. "I insist. I won't take no for an answer." Okay, so maybe *this* attractive man isn't such bad news. Perhaps his wife was fortunate enough to snag one of the good ones. In that case, there's no harm in being friendly.

I accept the gloves and slip my hands inside. "Thanks. I really didn't think this whole thing through." The people in front of us edge forward the slightest bit. Where do they think they're going? The doors are still just as closed as they were a minute earlier. Following the herd, the glove lender and I both take a step.

"So, what is it that your daughter wants that forced you to come here this morning?" I mean, I am wearing the man's gloves. I might as well be polite.

"I'm taking shopping advice from my brother-in-law." He shrugs. "Probably not a good idea, but I'm desperate. Apparently Madison saw something on TV that she just *has* to have. I'm pretty sure if I don't get it today, I won't have another chance."

"Ah, I see. She fell victim to a well-crafted holiday marketing campaign."

"Exactly. By this time next year, you won't be able to give these toys away, but for now, they're all anybody's talking about."

I nod. "Sounds like you're a good dad. Since you came out so early just to make your daughter happy, I hope you get what you came for."

"Me too."

❄

The minutes drag on, but eventually six o'clock comes and the doors open. I stay close behind my new acquaintance, my eyes level with his vest, until we reach the entrance. Once inside the store, the single-file line transforms into an unorganized mob. I suddenly feel like a salmon during spawning season, struggling alongside dozens of other fish veering this way and that. There's nowhere to go, yet for some reason everyone just keeps pushing. I glance to my left, where I find my rescuer. "It was nice meeting you," I call over the heads of the other shoppers.

"You too," he says with a wave. "Good luck on your quest."

"Thank you." I glance down at my hands and notice his gloves. "Oh, I almost forgot." I pull the gloves off and stretch my arm in front of a stern-faced older woman to return them. "Thanks again for these."

"No problem." He's nearly shouting over the noise.

Putting his handsome face out of my mind, I rein in my focus. It's time to find the TeddyTabs. They have to be in the toy department. Or might they be in electronics? Where either department is, I have no idea. I've never spent much time shopping in this store. The women's clothing department is to the left, and about a third of the customers separate from the larger group and head in that direction.

That eliminates a good portion of the competition. *Thank you, Lord.*

Cardboard aisle markers hang from the ceiling, suspended above the mass of bobbing heads, guiding us through the shoe department, then home decor. We have to be getting close. To my left, I catch sight of the man from outside, who, as he'd mentioned, is shopping for a toy as well. I keep him in my sights while maintaining a safe distance. No need to stalk him.

The uneasiness in my stomach grows as we round the corner. About half the remaining crowd banks right, toward the electronics department. Are they after the gaming console or the TeddyTab? The group that remains walking straight is still pretty large, so I take a chance and stay with them. Are all of these people after the same toy?

I spot the sign that reads Toys and Games. Others must notice it too, because all at once the crowd begins to walk faster. I glance at the handsome man who'd appeared calm and cool out on the sidewalk. He now has a worried look on his face. I'd maybe even call it panic-stricken. Should I be worried too? How many of these toys will be available? Hopefully enough for everyone who wants one.

After rounding the final corner, I halt swiftly to avoid running into the woman in front of me. Everyone has stopped. I stand on tiptoe to see what's causing the holdup. A crowd three rows deep has gathered around two pallets on the floor. Whatever is on those pallets is bound tightly in shrink wrap. Store employees scramble to uncover the loot and hand whatever it is to every impatient customer. Are they handing out TeddyTabs? Have I finally reached the pot of gold at the end of this horribly long rainbow?

The crowd begins to thin and people pass by me with boxes of TeddyTabs in hand and satisfied smiles on their faces. By the time I arrive in front of the pallets, one is already completely empty. The other has three—make that two—TeddyTab boxes on it. The aggressive older woman I encountered in the entryway grabs the second-to-last box and tosses it into her cart.

Finally. My turn has come. The last TeddyTab is mine.

I exhale in relief as I reach toward the box to stake my claim. But just as I grab it, another hand snatches the other end.

"Excuse me, but I was here first," a masculine voice says.

I look up and gasp. It's him. My knight in a navy blue vest.

# Daniel

The beautiful woman from the parking lot looks up in surprise, and my heart ping-pongs against my chest. Those crystal-blue eyes—the ones I found so captivating I could barely form a sentence—are now laser-focused on me, and the slanted brow above them is rather angry-looking.

We both rise to our full heights, still clutching opposite ends of the same box. I'm a good foot taller than her, but that doesn't seem to intimidate her. She tugs the box toward her. "You never said you were here for a TeddyTab."

I tighten my grip and try to pull it back my way. "Neither did you."

She notches her chin higher. "Well, this one's mine."

I clench my jaw, trying to remain calm and polite, yet assertive. This bear is the only thing Madison wants for Christmas, and I can't leave the store without it. "I'm sorry, but I got here before you did."

"What?" The woman's jaw drops. "I don't think so. I was next in line. You saw me step forward and reach for this box—"

"After I'd already put my hands on it."

"You did *not* have your hands on it until I had already grabbed it!" She glances over her shoulder, then huffs. "This is crazy.

Where are all the store clerks? There were three of them here a minute ago."

"Hey, that's a good idea," I say. "You should go and find someone to help you. I'm sure there are more of these bears in the back. I'll just take this one and get out of your way."

She shakes her head while pulling the box closer. "I have a better idea. I'll guard *my* bear while you flag down one of the employees."

I can only guess how silly we must look, each staking claim on the same teddy bear box. Thankfully the crowd around us has cleared so we no longer have an audience. "Are we just going to stand here like this all day?"

She shrugs. "We don't have to—if one of us would concede his rights to the bear."

"Oh, so now you're admitting that I have rights to it? I knew you'd come around eventually."

"Very funny." She rolls her eyes. "That's not what I meant. I'm only referring to your perceived rights to the bear, when in reality you have none."

"Oh, I see. So you're saying it's rightfully yours?"

Just then, a balding man wearing a red polo shirt embellished with the store logo rounds the corner.

The blond woman calls out, "Excuse me. Do you work here?"

"I do." He eyes us with one brow raised. "Can I help you two with something?"

She laughs, clearly trying to downplay the awkwardness of our situation. "Yes, thank you. We were wondering if you had any more of the TeddyTabs in your storeroom."

The clerk shakes his head. "I'm sorry, but we only received part of our shipment. We were lucky to get any at all. I hear they're sold out everywhere."

"I still don't understand what the big deal is," the woman says.

I have to say I agree with her on that point. Other than the fact that my daughter wants one and probably believes Santa is bringing her one, there really isn't anything that special about these bears, although the price tag suggests otherwise.

The clerk scratches his hairless head. "Beats me, ma'am, but they're flying off the shelves faster than any other toy this year."

I tip my head to the empty pallet. "When do you think you'll get more in?"

"The rest of our shipment was back-ordered until the thirty-first. This isn't typical Black Friday protocol, but I am authorized to issue a limited number of rain checks. Would you like one? You'd get the sale price."

Beside me, the woman sighs as though she's relieved. "The thirty-first? Well in that case, you can have this one." She releases the box and practically pushes it into my chest, then begins digging through her purse. "I will take a rain check, and I'll be back in five days to pick it up. Do I need to sign something?"

The clerk's nose wrinkles. "Five days?"

She tilts her head. "That's right. Today's the twenty-sixth, isn't it? And you said they'd be in on the thirty-first."

"Yes, the thirty-first of December. There is no thirty-first in November."

I watch as the color drains from the poor woman's face. "Oh. Right." She stuffs the pen back into her purse and zips it up.

"So ... do you still want that rain check?" the clerk asks.

The woman straightens, then releases a puff of air through her full lips. She glances briefly at me, almost as if she's giving me one last chance to concede, but when I don't, she turns back to the clerk. "Sure, I'll take it."

"Alrighty, then." The clerk pulls a pad of paper from his back pocket and begins jotting down numbers.

I wait for him to finish, just to make sure I don't leave the woman empty-handed. Well, she'll be empty-handed for now, but not forever. Meanwhile, she's glaring at me. I am definitely not her favorite person right now. But what can I do? I had one mission this morning, and this woman is the only thing standing in my way of accomplishing that mission. And yes, I do feel bad for taking the last bear, but not bad enough to give it up. It's for my daughter, whom I've known a *lot* longer than I've known this woman.

She edges closer to the clerk, turning her back on me. "While I wait for your next shipment, I'll search online. I'm sure I'll find another TeddyTab somewhere."

"Good luck with that." The clerk rips the slip of paper from the pad and hands it to her. "You can register this rain check on our website, and we'll notify you when the bear is back in stock." Then he nods and walks away.

Now it's just the two of us again. I dare to glance at her. The cheeks that had been devoid of color just a few moments ago are now full-blown red, and I'm starting to feel like a heel. "Look," I say, shoving my free hand in my vest pocket, "I didn't mean to upset you."

She takes a step back. "Upset me? I'm not the one who's going to be upset. You may have ruined my niece's Christmas. She's the one you should apologize to." With that, she turns and barrels toward the front of the store.

I stare after her for a few seconds, not sure what to do. One thing I do know is that I can't leave her feeling this way. I grasp the box with both hands and follow the determined woman down the aisle toward the exit. I pick up my pace until we're walking side by side. "Listen, I hope there are no hard feelings. After all, it's just a toy."

She stops mid-stride, then whips around to face me. "Just a toy? Then why couldn't you let me have it? It may be nothing to you, but it means an awful lot to my niece."

Suddenly feeling defensive, I grip the box tighter. "Well ... it means a lot to my daughter, too." At least I hope it will.

"I guess daughters trump nieces. Is that it?"

"Of course not. I never said that."

"I suppose if I were buying this toy for my own child, you'd be more sympathetic. But instead you're pulling rank because I'm *just* an aunt."

"Hey, wait a minute—"

She holds up her hand. "I don't want to fight with you. Enjoy your bear." With her chin raised, she clutches her purse to her side and leaves me standing slack-jawed in the middle of the store.

I can only stare after her, shaking my head. *Women.* Even after spending six years married to one, I'll never be able to figure them out.

I hug the box to my chest while I make my way to the checkout line. A band of remorse tightens around my middle the closer I get to the register. What came over me back there? My mind had been so set on buying Madison the perfect Christmas gift, I'd refused to back down until I got it—even at the expense of another person's feelings. A beautiful woman's feelings, no less. I'm such an idiot. This is not what Christmas is about.

*Lord, forgive me for forgetting why we're buying presents in the first place.*

After the cashier rings up my total, I slip my credit card into the chip reader and push the *OK* button on the keypad. With the receipt in hand, I dash through the sliding doors, hoping to catch the woman before she's gone.

The moment I step outside, I spot a black sedan weaving its way through the parking lot, toward the exit. I squint to see who's in the driver's seat. Sure enough, it's her. When she pulls out of the lane across from me, I jump in front of her vehicle. Her brakes screech as the car comes to a sudden stop.

The driver's side door swings open, and the woman jumps out. "What on earth are you doing?"

"I'm sorry." I hold my hands up in surrender as the shopping bag dangles from the crook of my arm. "My behavior in there was totally unacceptable. I don't know what got into me."

"I do. It's called an ego."

She sure isn't going to make this easy on me. "I have an idea." I offer my shopping bag to her. "Why don't you take the bear, and I'll take the rain check."

Her breath hitches. "Really?" Our gazes remain locked for a

moment before she blinks, then shakes her head. "No ... you know what? Give it to your daughter. I'm sure I'll be able to find one online."

"Are you sure?" I pull my wallet from my back pocket and remove one of my business cards. "Here. Take this. If you can't find a bear online, you can buy this one from me. Just give me a call. My offer stands through Christmas."

She hesitantly pulls the card from my fingers and examines it. "Thank you ... Daniel Hawkins." Her eyes meet mine as she says my name.

A car horn blares behind us. The woman jumps. "I'm blocking traffic." She scurries to her open door. "I appreciate the offer, but I don't want to be the reason your daughter doesn't get what she wants for Christmas. I know I'll find a TeddyTab somewhere. Let's just pretend today never happened."

"If you're sure."

"Very." She gives a single nod, slams her door, and speeds off.

I stand outside the store, staring after her car until it disappears. Forget today ever happened? Not possible. I may have single-handedly ruined Christmas for a little girl I've never met. Yet, for reasons I'm afraid to admit, it's the girl's aunt who concerns me the most.

# CHAPTER 6

# *Anna*

The bell above the front door jingles as I burst into the Suomi Art Center a little after eight. My shoulder sags under the weight of my tote as I close the door behind me. I let my bag slide down my arm until it hits the floor with a thud. "Sorry I'm late."

Carla, our program manager, emerges from the 2D studio, a small room behind the main exhibit hall where we hold painting and drawing classes several times a week. In one hand she grips an aluminum soup can full of paintbrushes while the other hand hugs a stack of drop cloths to her chest. Her harried expression worries me. Have I missed something?

"Where've you been?" Carla asks, her face flushed. "Laura Dunlap called in sick this morning and can't come in to teach the seniors' impressionism class. I've been doing the best I can to get things set up in there, but the ladies are getting restless." She nods toward the room she's just left. Loud female voices spill through the open door. "You know I'm no good with a paintbrush. I could never teach them the proper technique."

Carla's right. She got the job as project manager because of her excellent organizational and leadership skills—not her artistic talent. Between the two of us, I'm the only one capable of teaching the class. I run both hands through my long waves. "I'm sorry. I wouldn't have come late if I'd known. Let's just say I've had a rough morning."

"Ate too much turkey yesterday?"

A sad-sounding chuckle rumbles in my throat as I hurry to the front desk. "I wish. Actually I was shopping."

Carla's eyes bulge. "On Black Friday? You? I find that hard to believe."

"Believe me, it will never happen again." With a wave, I motion for Carla to join me at the computer. "I will teach the class if you do a favor for me."

"Anything."

I slide the mouse back and forth on the mouse pad. "I'm looking for something called a TeddyTab. Big Dealz is sold out, and apparently they're impossible to find. I've just spent the last hour and a half driving to every store in town, on the off chance that they actually did have TeddyTabs but failed to advertise them. No such luck. I need you to search for one online while I'm in class." My fingernails click against the keys as I open several webpages.

Carla peers over my shoulder. "Why do I get the feeling this has nothing to do with my job?"

"Because it doesn't." I tap my index finger on the mouse. "Look up every retail and auction site you can think of. Leave no search result unturned. Let me know if you find one and how much it costs."

Carla bobs her head. "I can do that." She glances up at me. "Wait, *why* would I do that?"

"It's a Christmas gift for Kelsey. I'll explain after class." I turn to the storage closet behind the front desk and open the door. A broom and dustpan fall to the floor. My jaw tightens as I suppress the angry outburst looming on the tip of my tongue. When was the last time someone bothered to clean out this closet?

Once I manage to find my white twill apron amidst the clutter, I loop the strap over my head and stop to take a calming breath. It isn't the messy closet that has my nerves frazzled. It's ... him.

*Relax, Anna. You'll never have to see that man—or his teddy bear—again.*

An hour later, I stand beside the glass front door and say goodbye to the last of my silver-haired art students. I blow my bangs from my forehead and then lean my head against the wall. My fingers are covered in paint, so I use my forearm to scratch an itch on my cheek. Then I turn to Carla and chuckle. "I'll tell you, those ladies kept me hopping. Viola Kleinhurst accused Nellie Campbell of copying her painting—as if the entire class wasn't copying Monet. Of course, Nellie Campbell was up in arms. For a minute I thought we might have a catfight on our hands."

"I would've paid money to see that." Carla's eyebrows bounce up and down.

I roll my eyes before returning to the studio to wash up in the utility sink. When I finally emerge paint-free, I join Carla by the computer. "How goes the search?"

Carla grimaces. "Not so well."

"You didn't find any?"

"Oh, I've found plenty." With a click of the mouse, Carla brings up several sites displaying images of TeddyTabs.

"There!" I shout, pointing to the screen.

"Don't get excited," Carla says. "Look at the prices."

I squint as she scrolls down to the bottom of the webpage. When she stops, my breath catches. "Five hundred dollars?"

"Yep. It's like that on every site. You can get a TeddyTab today —if you're willing to shell out big bucks."

"They're expensive enough as it is." I motion for Carla to step back, then I take control of the computer. "What about that discount warehouse site you love so much?"

"Temporarily out of stock. Order today and you'll receive one by January second."

I close my eyes and groan. "You're kidding me."

"Nope."

The sound of wind chimes echoes through the main gallery. It's my phone alerting me of a new text message.

"That reminds me," Carla says. "Your sister called. Twice. She said she's been trying to reach you for hours and you haven't answered. She wants to know if you got the bear."

Guilt roils in my gut. I've been avoiding Tamara's calls. "I meant to get back to her." But what would I say? I can't stand to let my sister down. Or Kelsey.

Carla pulls a second chair up to the desk and takes a seat. "So tell me what happened this morning that had you all riled up. And what's so special about this TeddyTab?"

I sigh. "It's a long story."

Carla makes a show of peering throughout the empty gallery. "I don't see anyone here. We have time to talk."

"All right." I take a deep breath. "I guess it all started with Thanksgiving dinner."

# CHAPTER 7

# *Daniel*

When I finally arrive at my office later that morning, I close my door, shove the shopping bag under my desk, and sigh in relief. One item checked off my single-daddy-at-Christmas checklist. Thank goodness Kurt had been in the living room yesterday, lying on the couch watching the Thanksgiving Day Parade with Madison while I slaved away in the kitchen. If not for his slothfulness, Kurt never would've caught on to Madison's excitement when the TeddyTab commercial came on.

Normally Kurt's lack of drive irks the tar out of me, but this time it actually paid off by helping me solve my gift-giving dilemma. Even with all the waiting and pushing, my morning was a success. I secured the sought-after bear.

Too bad I feel like I sold my soul for it.

Staring out the window of my second-floor office, I struggle to stay focused on work. Too many things are lobbying for my attention, and unfortunately, the one that's coming in last place is my latest project—a new central distribution center that will serve all four food banks in the tri-county area. The proposed location will be just outside of Lake Valley.

I rub my tired eyes with the heels of my hands. How can I

concentrate when the image of the blond-haired beauty from Big Dealz runs through my mind every minute? I'd been quite taken with her from the moment we met in the parking lot—before she became the one thing standing between Madison and her TeddyTab.

And that's a bit unsettling. Actually, it's *really* unsettling. I haven't had a single romantic thought about anyone since Leah. Women come in and out of my office on a daily basis. I sit through meetings with them, go to business lunches with them, and discuss projects with them. I'm not affected in the least. Madison's first grade teacher is a woman about my age, but do I want to date her? No. I can't even remember her name.

Okay, it's Ms. Snyder, but I only know that because Madison talks about her almost every day. The point is, I don't care what her name is. I'm not looking to get involved with someone. Yet this morning, when I pulled that poor woman up in the parking lot and our eyes met, all the sensory switches in my brain were flipped to high alert. My pulse raced. My stomach felt queasy.

And then all I felt was ... guilt. How could I have that kind of reaction to a total stranger? My heart's taken. It belongs to Leah and always will. She's the one God chose for me—the *only* one. End of discussion.

I spin around in my chair and gaze out the window at the street below, then release a long sigh. No matter how devoted I was to my wife and still continue to be, the awful truth remains— Leah is gone. And at twenty-nine, I have a lot of life left to live. Would she really expect me to live out my remaining years alone? After almost two years without my wife, could these weird, unwelcome feelings be my heart's way of telling me it's okay to move on?

I shudder at the thought. I don't feel ready, and I don't know if I ever will be. Reentering the dating game is a big step. Not that it matters now, after I was so rude to the woman at the store. She wouldn't want anything to do with me even if I *did* decide I wanted to pursue her.

Grinding my jaw, I turn away from the window and stare down at the sketches on the table, the lines blurring into a jumbled mess of black and white. A few more unproductive minutes pass before I force a breath and roll up the drawings so I can bring them to the boardroom. Several members of the Northern Minnesota Food Bank's board of directors are on their way to review the detailed design plans for the distribution center.

I'm so relieved to finally be moving on to the next phase of this project. During concept design, everything I came up with failed to meet the expectations of the executive director, Alvin Reed. Building one central distribution center has been the man's passion for years, and it's finally becoming a reality. Unfortunately, his grandiose plans did not fall within the budget he allowed. Over the last several weeks, he's had to let go of a few nonessential elements, while I've had to go in a different direction with my subsequent sketches. Compromise has been the theme of this project.

But I think I have a final, detailed design that we can all agree on. If not, I might have to scrap the whole thing and start over. Worse—I could lose this job altogether. I pray it won't come to that. I'm lucky to have acquired this project. Being a sole practitioner in a small-town architecture firm with so many big-name firms just a couple of hours away in Minneapolis, I need this job to survive in such a competitive market.

And speaking of survival, only an extra dose of caffeine will help me survive what is sure to be a long meeting. I reach for my stainless steel mug and down the last of my coffee. On my way out the door, I stop and silently petition God for a chance to redeem myself in the eyes of the woman I met at the store. I may not be ready to start dating again, but that doesn't mean I want her to think of me as a self-centered bully, either. I just want to do the right thing by her, not marry her. In a town of only ten thousand people, we're bound to run into each other again. Is it too much to ask for a second chance to make a first impression?

# CHAPTER 8

# Anna

It's late Saturday morning. I'm at the mall, standing inside Lake Valley's one and only dress shop holding two dresses by their hangers, one in my right hand and one in my left. "Which one is more appropriate for a small-town, up-north, not-for-profit art gallery? The black or the ivory?"

Tamara takes two steps toward me and plucks both hangers from my grasp. "Neither." She returns both dresses to the rack. "This isn't a funeral, and you're not getting married. Art directors need something with a bit more color." She tilts her head and peers at me, scrutinizing. "Although seeing you in a wedding dress wouldn't be a bad thing."

I can feel my jaw tighten. "Please stay focused. I need a dress for tonight." If this event were taking place at the museum where I worked in Seattle, which was one of the biggest art museums in the Pacific Northwest, I'd have a dozen outfits that would be more than appropriate. But this isn't Seattle, and I no longer work at a large, metropolitan museum. I work at a small art center that supports Minnesota artists. The people in this town are laid-back, casual. I don't want to overdress—but at the same time, tonight's event is a fundraiser, and many of the guests will be important people from the community, so I don't want to underdress either.

I want to look like I fit in here, which sounds crazy because I grew up here. Of course I should fit in. But after almost seven years away, including college and the three years I spent out west, I feel like the town and everyone in it has moved on without me.

The sound of a door swinging open and slamming against the wall snaps me out of my reverie.

"Ta-da!" Kelsey bursts out of the dressing room nearly tripping over the pink bridesmaid's gown she's wearing. Not surprising, since it's over two feet too long for her. It's adorned with sequins and enough tulle to mosquito-proof the entire state of Minnesota.

Tamara gasps. "Take that off this minute!"

Stifling a laugh, I cover my mouth with my hand.

Kelsey gallops through the store, keeping just out of her mother's reach. I shake my head at my niece's antics. The girl could use a little more discipline, but I have to admit it's good to see her laugh.

While Tamara tries to rein in her daughter, I turn back to the matter at hand—finding a dress for tonight's auction. The doors open at five for patrons who want to mingle and view the featured photographs prior to bidding, and it's already nearing lunchtime. There's no time to waste. Ignoring Tamara's comments about the ivory dress, I pull it free from the hanger and march toward the cashier. If I put a belt around the middle, add a strand of colorful beads, and wear a denim or leather jacket, no one will mistake me for a bride.

Once Kelsey is dressed in her own clothes, I lead the way out of the store and into the mall's wide corridor. The aroma of fresh-baked cookies fills the air as we pass the food court.

Kelsey bounces on her toes. "I want a chocolate chip cookie!"

I quicken my pace. "We don't have time for a snack break. Auntie Anna has a big night ahead of her." I wave my sister and niece on toward the mall's main entrance. At least I think that's where we're headed. Only, I don't remember passing the coffee kiosk when we entered an hour earlier. Or the lingerie store.

"This isn't the way we came in," Tamara says.

I rub the back of my neck. "I realize that now." I quickly survey our surroundings and start in the other direction, then freeze when Kelsey lets out a squeal. The little girl shouts something about elves and takes off running.

Tamara charges after her daughter.

Helpless, I stand on tiptoes, peering down the crowded corridor until I spot two giant candy canes on either side of a sparkling red-and-green hut.

Santa's Village.

I groan. "Anything but that." If Kelsey gets a chance to sit on Santa's lap, she'll ask for the one gift she can't have—a TeddyTab. Sure, I've secured a rain check, but every kid in America knows Santa doesn't deliver presents on December thirty-first. If only I'd been more aggressive like every other Black Friday shopper. Then maybe I'd have the bear already.

The image of a frustratingly handsome man holding a bear that should've been mine flashes through my mind. With Santa's Village in my sights, I start running. I have to stop Kelsey from speaking to Santa and getting her hopes up more than they already are.

Unfortunately, I seem to have misjudged both the length of the corridor and my physical stamina. Halfway to Santa's Village, I have to pause and catch my breath. Not to mention, my strappy heels are not cut out for sprinting. "Kelsey, wait!" I flail my arms in a pathetic attempt to capture my niece's attention, but it's no use. Kelsey is already closing in on the big man in red.

When I finally arrive at the fake North Pole, Kelsey is seated on Santa's lap.

Tamara is standing beside the raised platform with her hand to her heaving chest. "I couldn't catch her. She's too fast."

I exhale a whoosh of air. "She takes after her father." He's good at running away.

Santa pats a beaming Kelsey on the knee. "And what is your name?"

"Kelsey."

"It's so nice to see you, Kelsey. Have you been a good girl this year?"

"Yes." She nods excitedly.

Ha! I could list several incidents from the past hour alone that would greatly challenge that answer.

Santa chuckles in his jolly fashion while placing his white-gloved hand to his belly. "What can I bring you this year?"

"A TeddyTab." Not even a hint of hesitation.

Santa's smile flattens. He shifts his questioning gaze to Tamara, who winks and nods her approval.

"What are you doing?" I whisper to my sister. "You just told Santa he could promise Kelsey a TeddyTab."

"And he will. You got one, didn't you?"

Guilt bores a hole through my conscience. "I did ... for the most part. But it won't arrive until after Christmas."

"What?" Tamara's outburst turns the heads of parents and children around us.

"Shh." I place a hand on her shoulder. "I didn't get a chance to tell you. The bear is back-ordered, but I have a rain check."

"You had all day yesterday to tell me. Is that why you ignored my calls?"

I'm so ashamed. I want to crawl behind Santa's red velvet throne and hide there for the rest of the day. "I'm sorry. I wasn't sure how to tell you. I didn't want to let you down."

Kelsey hops down from Santa's lap with a huge grin plastered on her face and a holiday coloring book in her hands. "I can't wait 'til Christmas!"

I cringe. This epic failure is sure to put me on Santa's naughty list for the rest of my life.

*Daniel*

I lift Madison up to the glass case for a better look. "What kind of cookie do you want?"

"Chocolate chip."

"Good choice." After ordering the oversized treat, I take my daughter by the hand and lead her away from the other temptations in the food court. Heaven help me if she catches sight of the place that sells those gooey cinnamon rolls.

A twinge of guilt ties my stomach in knots. I've caved again. Leah never would've allowed our daughter to have a cookie so close to lunchtime—especially not one so big. Am I honoring my wife's memory and the values she tried to instill in our daughter by giving in every time Madison asks for something? It's a challenging spot to be in, acting as both mother and father to a six-year-old girl. The question *What would Leah do?* tugs at me in every situation. More often than not, Daddy's little girl gets her way.

I glance at Madison's chocolate-smeared cheeks and chuckle. Maybe I'm overanalyzing things. She won't be little forever. There will only be so many opportunities to spoil her with cookies and dates at the mall. Hopefully Leah would understand.

I hand Madison a napkin for her messy fingers. "So, what should we get Uncle Kurt for Christmas?"

"A hamster."

I barely hold in my laughter. "Why a hamster?"

"Because Uncle Kurt's all alone. He needs something to keep him company, and hamsters are fun! They run around and around in their hamster wheels all day."

True, Kurt does need company, but I think the company of a good woman would be preferable to that of a hamster. At least a woman could motivate him to get serious about his life. A hamster—well, like Madison said, they just run in circles, and Kurt's already doing that.

I rub my hand across my jaw. "We'll find a gift for Uncle Kurt later. What about Grandma Bev? I was thinking we could get her a gift card to that cactus farm in Tucson that she loves so much. I don't want to get her anything too big, since we have to mail her gift."

Madison scrunches her nose. "Cactuses are ugly—and too spikey. Grandma needs a kitten. They're way softer, and better to snuggle with."

Huh? "What is it with you and pets today?" Is Madison trying to tell me something? We have no pets. Would she like a puppy for Christmas more than the TeddyTab? I know of at least one woman in town who would gladly take the electronic bear off my hands—with a little encouragement. If only I knew her name or where she works. Why hadn't I asked her? Oh, right, because she couldn't get away from me fast enough.

"Santa!" Madison's grip on my hand tightens. She tugs on my arm and points at something on the other end of the corridor. "Daddy, look."

I swivel my head in the direction of Madison's open-mouthed stare and catch sight of a large cardboard house that's supposed to look like it's made of candy.

"Can we go?"

I draw my phone from my pocket and check the time. Eleven thirty. "Sure, why not?"

My little girl claps with glee and dashes in the direction of Santa's Village.

"Slow down!" As I follow after her, a girl no taller than Madison, her head buried in the pages of a book, runs smack into my legs. She falls back and lands flat on her behind.

"I'm sorry," I say as I stoop to help her up. "Are you all right?"

"She'll be fine."

The feminine voice draws my attention upward. When my

gaze settles on wheat-blond hair and sky-blue eyes, my heart races. I rise to my full height while pulling the little girl to her feet. "It's you," I say.

I hear her breath hitch. Her eyes grow wide as realization dawns on her face. "It's ... *you*."

CHAPTER 9

*Anna*

The second my sights land on Daniel Hawkins, the man I've been trying and failing to shove out of my mind for over twenty-four hours, my insides flame with heat. My outsides, however, freeze in place. He's standing before me like a hero, having just helped Kelsey up, similar to the way he helped me in the parking lot after I'd landed in a puddle of slush.

I guess we know where Kelsey gets her lack of coordination.

What is Daniel doing at the mall at the exact time I'm here? Lake Valley may be a small town, but isn't it big enough for the two of us to exist without running into each other two days in a row? Especially today, which is a very important day for the Suomi Art Center. The last thing I need as the new executive art director is something—or someone—clouding my focus.

I steel myself against Daniel's charm, his delicious brown eyes, and force a smile. "Thank you for helping my niece." I tug on Kelsey's arm, pulling her close. "Now if you'll excuse us, we have to get home."

"But Mommy's still in the bathroom."

I groan. Tamara and her tiny, unpredictable bladder! "All right, let's go find your mommy." I tip my head in Daniel's direction. "Have a nice day."

"Wait." He grasps my shoulder, stopping me. "Don't you think this is crazy, us running into each other again?"

Crazy? That's one word to describe it, but I'm leaning a bit more toward *humiliating.* It's like in high school, when I finally got up the nerve to tell my chemistry lab partner that I was crushing on him, only for him to flat-out reject me and then laugh about it with his friends. Okay, so maybe the two experiences aren't nearly the same, but the point is, I didn't exactly feel comfortable sitting next to that guy and sharing a Bunsen burner with him for the rest of the semester.

Just like I don't feel comfortable being around the very handsome Daniel Hawkins only a day after behaving like a crazed lunatic at Big Dealz. *Ugh.*

Daniel takes a step forward, and I realize that his hand is still on my shoulder. "I've actually been hoping to get the chance to talk to you about yesterday, but I never thought I'd—"

"Where were you guys?" Tamara's voice rises above the noisy background chatter as she makes her way toward us. "I told you to wait outside the restroom." Her eyes land on Daniel, and she stops mid-stride. With her jaw hanging open like a largemouth bass, she does a double take. "Anna, aren't you going to introduce me to your friend?"

Could this day get any worse? I gesture to Daniel. "Tamara, this is Mr. Hawkins. He and I met yesterday."

"Sounds intriguing. Please, tell me more." Tamara's voice is dripping with sweetness.

Daniel clears his throat. "Um, actually, we met at Big Dealz. We were both shopping for one of those—"

I fling my arm into his chest, catching him mid-sentence and nearly knocking him off balance. "Dresses!" I shout. "We were both shopping for dresses." I hold up my garment bag as proof of my tiny white lie. "I finally found one. How 'bout you, Mr. Hawkins?"

His brows knit together. "What?"

I nod my head toward my niece and shoot Daniel a wide-eyed

look of warning. Hadn't he done enough to ruin Kelsey's Christmas without mentioning her intended gift out loud?

Tamara's eyebrows meet in a deep *V*. "Seems to me, Anna, you would've told me about meeting someone like Mr. Hawkins."

Tingling heat creeps up my neck. "I'm sorry, I had a lot on my mind." Mostly, Daniel Hawkins. I extend my hand toward the man, who's looking slightly bewildered. "We really should be going," I tell him. "I have a big evening ahead of me. Lots to do."

His eyes seem to search mine. "Yeah, I'd better go too. My daughter's standing in line waiting to see Santa." As he accepts my outstretched hand, his thumb brushes against my knuckles.

Tingles race up my arm, and my heart beats five times in rapid succession. It does the same thing when I've had too much caffeine, only I haven't had a drop of coffee this morning. I'll consider it a delayed reaction to *yesterday's* coffee, because there's no way my body is that jumpy over Daniel simply touching my hand.

Once we're outside, I try to stay one step ahead of Tamara to avoid the questions I know are coming, but my aching feet slow me down.

"What was that all about?" Tamara's voice broadcasts across the parking lot.

Next time I go shopping, I'm wearing sneakers. "What was *what* about?"

Even with Kelsey in tow, Tamara is faster than me. She catches up and jabs her thumb toward the mall behind us. "In there. With Mr. Gorgeous. Why did you treat him like that?"

Frustration surges through my veins. "I was perfectly cordial."

"You were rude. Did you not *see* the man?"

We cross the parking lot, and my sedan comes into view. I click my key fob, unlocking the doors. "Of course I saw him."

"And?"

Another click of a button opens the trunk. When I reach my car, I toss my garment bag inside. "And what? He's married. You heard him, he has a daughter."

"I didn't see a ring."

"You looked?" I whip my head around. Of course she looked. She's always trying to set me up with eligible bachelors. I slam the trunk. "Anyway, the lack of a ring doesn't prove anything. Maybe he's one of those unfortunate men who has a gold allergy and can't wear a ring. Or maybe he works in a lumber mill, and he doesn't want to lose a finger when his ring gets caught on a piece of machinery." Never mind the fact that I already know, thanks to the business card he gave me, that he's an architect. Telling Tamara that will only weaken the case I've mounted against him.

Tamara angles her head to one side. "I seriously doubt he has a gold allergy. And if he had a dangerous job, he'd wear one of those rubber rings or have a tattoo around his finger. Believe me, I saw the way he looked at you, and that man is interested."

My fingers tighten around my key chain. How exactly did Daniel look at me? And why is my heart suddenly racing?

"I think you should try to get his number," Tamara says as she opens the back passenger door.

"That makes zero sense." I squeeze myself between my car and one beside it that parked way too close. "After what happened between you and Wayne—and me and Brady, for that matter—you should probably encourage me to be careful, not to chase after a guy I barely know." Besides, I already have Daniel's number, but *no way* am I calling it. I lift the handle and ease my door open.

Tamara straightens, then frowns at me across the car's roof. "You're seriously comparing that fine specimen of a man in there to Wayne? Not every good-looking guy is a commitment-phobe with wandering eyes, Anna. And I know that Brady's betrayal completely blindsided you, but there are still decent men in this world, and you're going to miss out if you judge them all before getting to know them."

I lower myself into my seat while Tamara buckles Kelsey in the back. While I wait for my sister to claim the passenger seat, I attempt to push all thoughts of Daniel from my mind. I don't want to think about him. Thinking about him makes me have all kinds of feelings that I don't want to feel right now. It'd be so much easier if he had one of those giant moles on the tip of his nose with a big black hair growing out of it, or maybe a few missing teeth right in the front. Then I definitely wouldn't give him a second thought. Or a third or fourth thought, which seems to be my pattern. Tonight I need to keep my thoughts focused on the auction. And my job. That's what matters. Oh, and finding Kelsey a TeddyTab—a *different* TeddyTab, totally unrelated to the one that Daniel has. There are too many bad memories associated with that one.

I force myself to take a deep breath, then blow out a steady stream of air. Everything will be fine. I'll go home, get ready for the auction, and pray I never see Daniel Hawkins again.

# Daniel

I enter a dimly lit Suomi Art Center just before six, arriving at the tail end of social hour. The front room is abuzz with the low murmur of patrons conversing while sipping from fluted glasses and snacking on small plates of hors d'oeuvres. I pass through the crowd into the main gallery, where I take a moment to admire the photographs displayed on the stark-white walls. I only plan to stay a little while—just long enough to make an appearance and represent the firm. An hour should be more than enough time to shake hands and rub elbows with the right people. Hopefully I can escape before the bidding gets underway. Then I can go home and rescue my daughter from her Uncle Kurt, who really has no business babysitting at all. He has the emotional maturity of a second grader. Maybe that's why he and Madison get along so well.

I shake off the thought as I wander through the main gallery and into a smaller one. In the center of this room, on a free-standing easel lit up by spotlights, sits a stunning black-and-white print of a mother and her two young sons standing in front of what looks like a small garden plot. The mother is holding a glove-covered hand to her forehead. She looks exhausted. I pause a moment to admire the picture. It's truly striking.

From behind me comes the sound of someone tapping on a microphone, drawing my attention to the raised platform situated along one wall of the main gallery. A momentary blast of feedback echoes throughout the room. Alvin Reed, whom I'd met with the day before to discuss the distribution center project, stands behind a podium.

"Good evening." As Mr. Reed speaks, silence falls upon the small crowd gathering near the makeshift stage. "Thank you all for joining us to support this collaborative endeavor and bring attention to a growing concern in our community." The rotund man reaches for a glass of water on a stand beside the podium and takes a sip.

"As many of you know, last week was National Hunger and Homelessness Awareness Week. Even in a community as small as Lake Valley, we're no strangers to these serious issues. Far too many of our people are forced to forgo the luxury of food or housing in order to pay for other critical expenses. Every day, volunteers work tirelessly at the homeless shelter, which is currently located in St. Margaret's Church, but due to limited space and an outdated facility, many of those seeking shelter are turned away. Meanwhile, our local food bank, which is the hub for the northern Minnesota district, isn't big enough to hold and distribute the amount of food necessary to feed all those in need. While we're thankful to have these facilities, lack of space is a major concern, which is why planning is underway for a new food pantry distribution center. Yes, this is a big undertaking, but fundraising efforts have been underway for over a year, and we're close to meeting our goal. Through your generous support of this auction tonight, we'll be that much closer to covering the enormous cost of this new building project."

He steps away from the podium for a minute and motions to someone in the shadows. "And now, to tell us a little more about these photographs, I'd like to welcome the co-chair of this event, the new executive art director of the Suomi Art Center."

Now my interest is piqued. I've never been one to frequent

the local gallery, but I've heard talk of a new art director on staff. I don't recall the name of the person. Curious, I crane my neck to see who it is, but the crowd around me is pressing in, blocking my view of the podium.

Mr. Reed extends his arm. "Please welcome Miss Anna McAllister."

*Anna.* I step to the side, away from the colossal man in front of me, and catch sight of the woman who has occupied my thoughts for the past thirty-some hours. So she works at the gallery? I almost laugh. This is too good—I can't believe my luck. No, *luck* isn't the word. It's more than that. It's providence. God is definitely smiling on me tonight.

*Anna*

I jump when Carla elbows me in the ribs.

"Go on. He's waiting."

"Already?" I was hoping Mr. Reed would live up to his reputation for being long-winded and talk for just a few more minutes.

When everyone around me begins to clap, I gulp a breath and make my way to the podium. Mentally reciting my prepared words as I walk, I join Mr. Reed, accept the handheld microphone, and turn to face the crowd with a smile.

That's when my hands start shaking.

I clear my throat before forcing the words from my mouth. "I'd like to thank each of you for joining us here tonight. Your very presence demonstrates your concern for those in need, and on behalf of the Suomi Art Center, I'd like to show my appreciation." I lead the group in a quick round of applause while scanning the faces before me. Most of the members of the art center's board of directors are in attendance, as well as our studio manager and other part-time employees. But there are also a lot of unfamiliar faces. Even though I grew up in this town, a lot of new people have moved into the community during my absence. I do recognize some of the guests as local business owners, their employees, and volunteers at the Lake Valley Food Bank. I've gotten to know them over the last few weeks while organizing this charity event.

When the clapping ceases, I continue. "As Mr. Reed mentioned, we're here to raise money for a much-needed central distribution center to serve our area food banks. The subjects in the photographs you will be bidding on tonight represent a cross section of the food-insecure population in not only our small town, but several surrounding counties."

A throat clears loudly from somewhere in the back of the crowd. I swivel my head to follow the sound and stop cold when a familiar face catches my eye.

Daniel Hawkins.

My stomach flips while heat rushes to my cheeks. I suddenly struggle to find my voice. "The ... um ..." The words of my speech flee my mind like a bird through an open window. I swallow, fighting to regain control. "The ... photographs on these walls were taken by ..." *Oh no. What is the photographer's name?*

My palm suddenly sweaty, I clench the microphone tighter, praying it doesn't slip out of my hand. I steal another glance at Daniel, and my head begins to spin. What is he doing here? I place my free hand on the podium to steady myself.

*Come on, Anna. Just remember your speech.*

I gulp, hoping to loosen anxiety's tight hold on my throat. "For the entire month of November, the Suomi Art Center has been proudly displaying the photographs of ... Grant Deluso. Yes! Grant Deluso, renowned artist and recipient of the prestigious Ashton Fellowship." Did my voice just crack? "We hope the forty portraits that make up our 'Faces of Hunger' exhibit will shed some light on the harsh reality of many of our area's residents."

Now I think I'm suffering from a bad case of dry mouth. If I only had some water—oh, thank goodness. Someone set a glass of water on a stand beside the podium. "Excuse me for a moment." I reach for the glass and take a sip. Only after I swallow do I recall Alvin Reed drinking from the very same glass. I try to hide my grimace as I set the water down.

This is not happening. None of this is happening. It's only a dream.

*Please, God, let this all be a dream.*

I can feel perspiration running down the back of my neck as I struggle to recall my closing remarks. "After looking at the men, women, and children in these photographs, we can no longer ignore this problem. Each of the prints has been sponsored by one of several local businesses, all of whom have pledged to match the price of the winning bids up to a maximum of five hundred dollars. By purchasing one of these prints tonight, you will take the first step toward putting food on the tables of some of these precious people." I offer the crowd a perfunctory smile. "And now let me introduce the photographer himself to tell you about the inspiration behind the project. Please welcome Mr. Grant Deluso."

Once the applause dies down, I back away from the podium, hand Mr. Deluso the mic, and make a beeline for the ladies' room. Will anyone notice if I spend the rest of the evening in hiding?

I slip through the crowd, praying no one will try to stop me, when a hand gently grasps my upper arm. Panic seizes my chest as I turn around, but a sense of relief overtakes it when I see Carla's face, not Daniel's. "Where are you off to in such a hurry?" Carla asks.

"What do you mean?" I grab her shoulders and duck, using her body as a shield. Anything to stay out of Daniel's line of sight.

"What's wrong with you?"

"Nothing. I'm fine. Why?"

"Well, during your speech you seemed a little ... off."

I wince. "Was it that noticeable?"

"I would say so. You look like you need to sit down for a while."

I clap my hands. "That's perfect! I'm headed to the ladies' room. I'll just ... sit in there."

She grimaces. "Please spare me the details."

With a nervous chuckle, I wave off Carla's concerns. "Go mingle. I'll be right back." I sidle past several unoccupied benches on my way toward the back of the building. Turning right, I exit the small gallery and duck into the restroom. Inside, I lean my back against the wall and take deep, calming breaths until my heart rate slows to its normal rhythm.

I need to chill. This is a big night for the art center, an important event for the community, and I can't let Daniel Hawkins turn me into a lunatic. Besides, even though he clearly saw me, he may not have recognized me. We've only met once. No, twice— not that it matters.

I step to the sink, turn on the faucet, and fill my palms with water. After taking several gulps, I let the water seep through my fingers. Then I stare into the mirror. I can do this. I can walk back into the exhibit hall and mingle with the guests like nothing happened, like I didn't almost lose all motor function up on that stage. I have *totally* got this. After drying my hands on a paper towel, I fluff my hair and lift my chin high.

I confidently exit the restroom, round the corner, and slam into a rock wall. Or what feels like a rock wall, only not as cold. I open my eyes and wait for my vision to clear. Do rock walls usually wear navy blue sport jackets?

"I'm sorry," a familiar voice says while strong hands take hold of my shoulders. "You okay there?"

Still slightly dazed, I look up into Daniel's face. *Not again.* The overhead track lights begin to spin. I place a hand to the wall to steady myself. "I'm perfectly fine." Or I will be, when the little yellow lights stop twinkling in my periphery.

"I was hoping I'd run into you." His lips form a crooked smile. "Only, not literally."

Once the spinning in my head subsides, I push against the wall, relieving it of its supportive duties, and stand straight and tall. "Please don't take this the wrong way," I say, "but I was kind of hoping the opposite."

His smile instantly flattens. "Why?"

What can I say that won't hurt his feelings or make me look like some lovesick teenager who's struggling to keep her hormones in check? Truth be told, Daniel Hawkins is just plain dangerous. To my heart. And when a person encounters a dangerous situation, like a burning building, for example, she doesn't run *into* the fire—she runs away from it. And that's exactly what I'm doing. Daniel is a fire, and I don't want to get burned.

I gaze down at my bare wrist, then tuck my hand behind my back. "Oh, wow. I didn't realize it had gotten so late. I have to get back to the guests."

His brow wrinkles. "You're not wearing a watch."

I chuckle. "I don't need one. I can sense the time. If you thought giving speeches was my *only* talent, you would be sorely mistaken." Then, like a hitchhiker on the side of the road, I jab my thumb toward the exhibit hall. "Duty calls."

"Wait, Anna—"

Ignoring Daniel's plea, I hurry away as quickly as I can in heels, making it a full five feet only to be stopped by Alvin Reed.

He raises his hands toward both Daniel and me in greeting. "Just the two people I was looking for."

*Oh no.* What could he possibly want with the two of us?

# CHAPTER 11

# Daniel

Alvin Reed must've been a linebacker in his younger years. He wraps his arm around my back and clasps my bicep, pulling me into what can only be described as an awkward side hug that nearly knocks me off balance.

"I was on my way to introduce the two of you," the boisterous man says, "but I see you already know each other."

I politely shrug out of his hold, then brush the wrinkles from my coat sleeves. I cast a side glance at Anna. "We're ... *getting* to know each other."

A blush spreads across Anna's cheeks. She gives Alvin a lopsided half smile and splays her hands. "We've run into each other. Several times."

"Wonderful," says Alvin. "Then you might know that Daniel is the lead architect on the distribution center project."

Anna's gaze flits toward me. "I did *not* know that. That's ... impressive."

"Thank you." Any praise at all is good coming from Anna. From what I've experienced so far, she doesn't hand it out freely.

Next Alvin gestures toward Anna. "And we owe the success of tonight's exhibit to this visionary young lady right here. These black-and-white portraits—what a powerful way to cut out all distractions and shed some light on what really matters."

She shifts her weight from one leg to the other while biting her lip. I can't tell if she's looking for an escape route out of this conversation or if she's had too much punch. "To be honest," she says with a tilt of her head, "I can't take any credit for this exhibit or the auction. The last executive director sent out a call for art in the spring before his retirement. He planned out the entire year's worth of exhibits at that time. It was actually Mr. Deluso himself who came up with the idea for the 'Faces of Hunger' exhibit. When I started working here in mid-September, I simply fell into the project while it was already in the works."

"I see. My mistake," Alvin says.

Anna frowns, then straightens her spine and squares her shoulders. "Well, you see, you're not exactly mistaken, because I do agree with you, it's a brilliant idea. Part of me wishes I *had* come up with it on my own—not that I need the validation or anything. I mean, what other causes are more deserving than hunger and homelessness? I recently moved back here from Seattle, so I'm no stranger to the reality that exists in other parts of the country, but to find out that people in our own small community are struggling with these issues ... it's been quite a wake-up call." She stops talking suddenly, looks at Alvin, then me, and grimaces. "Sorry, I'm rambling. Am I rambling?"

"A little?" I say, not wanting to hurt her feelings. But seriously, I don't think she's taken a breath in two straight minutes. Does she always talk this much or is she nervous? Is it because of Alvin Reed ... or me?

I offer her my most sincere smile. "The world would be a better place if more people cared for those less fortunate and actually did something about it."

She looks down as a blush covers both her cheeks.

"I'm glad you feel that way, Daniel," Alvin says. After placing a hand on each of our shoulders, he draws us into a huddle. "Now that I have the two of you together, I'd like to run an idea by you.

As executive director of the food bank, I get very busy during the holiday season, as I'm sure you can imagine. One responsibility I'd like to hand to someone else would be overseeing the children's holiday gift program."

"Gift program?" Anna repeats.

Alvin nods. "Each year the food bank teams up with the county's Child and Family Services office to provide holiday meal boxes for those living in food-insecure households, along with gifts for each of the children in those families. I'm sure you've seen the Christmas trees we've placed in several local department stores and banks this holiday season—the ones with the paper gingerbread people hanging from them?"

Anna looks sheepishly at the man. "To be honest, I've only been shopping twice in the past few weeks, and both times I had ... *other things* on my mind. I'm afraid I didn't notice any trees." Her gaze swings toward me, and she lifts her brow.

I'm about to come to my own defense when Alvin waves a hand through the air. "No matter," he says. "It's simple. Each paper ornament represents a real boy or girl in the community whose parents qualify for the food assistance program. We have the parents fill out a questionnaire listing their child's age, clothing size, hobbies and interests, then assign a paper ornament to each child. We hang those ornaments up on the different trees we've set up across town. Patrons can select a child, shop for him or her, and drop their gifts in a bag with the paper ornament attached into the donation boxes we've placed beside each tree."

"That sounds like a great idea," Anna says. "But what happens if there are ornaments left over? Do those children go without gifts?"

Mr. Reed shakes his head. "Oh, no. We send volunteers out to shop for every child whose ornaments were not selected, just to ensure that no one is left out. Our volunteers sort the items toward the middle of December, and they'll distribute them along with the holiday food boxes a few days before Christmas at the food bank." He leans in. "This year, two of our regular volunteers had to bow out at the last minute for personal reasons, and I'm afraid we'll be struggling to get all the gifts picked up and sorted. But with you two caring individuals involved, I think we could get it done in a very organized fashion."

"So this is just a limited commitment?" I ask. "You're not looking for anything beyond the holidays?"

Alvin shrugs. "After we distribute the gifts, there will be no further commitment. Maybe down the road a vacancy will open up on the food bank board of directors, and you'll feel led to run. If so, I would be glad to have you on board. But for now, all I'm looking for is some help with the gift program. I don't want it to fall by the wayside. The kids really look forward to it, and their families are counting on us."

Anna bites her lip again. "Do you really need both of us to help? Or could one of us do the job?"

"Both of you would be preferred," Alvin replies. "I've lost two volunteers, and I'd like to replace them both."

She leans in further toward the man. "Would we ever need to be in the same place at the same time?" Her voice isn't much above a whisper, but I can still make out every word.

Alvin pats her on the back and chuckles. "Well, it certainly would make things easier if you were." He smiles down at her. "Just think about it, that's all I'm asking. But don't take too long to decide. I'll be holding a short meeting this Thursday night at six for volunteers. I'd love to see you both there."

Anna's index finger shoots up as she clears her throat. "Um … my niece has dance class on Thursday nights. If my sister's working, I'm responsible for getting her to and from class."

Alvin waves her concern away. "No problem. Just come by after you drop her off. If you need to leave early, that's fine too."

"Okay, but if my sister *doesn't* work, then … oh. Well, in that case I would be able to come." Her cheeks redden, and she looks down at the floor.

I'm guessing Anna hopes she's busy Thursday night. The woman has an obvious aversion to the idea of working with me on this project, and I'm pretty sure I know why—she's still upset about Black Friday. Call me a glutton for punishment, but I really want to work with her. I think it'd be a great opportunity for us to get to know each other without the pressure that comes with going on an actual date—not that she'd say yes to an actual date with me. So I step up to the plate. "I think this program sounds like a great idea, sir." I extend my hand toward Alvin. "You can count me in."

A huge grin breaks out across the man's face as he grabs my hand in both of his, giving it a vigorous shake. "I'm glad to hear that." He bobs his head toward Anna. "If you two help out, it will really lessen the burden from the other volunteers." Alvin winks as he backs away. "Now I'll let you two chat while I check out these remarkable photographs."

Anna steps forward and reaches for Mr. Reed. "Wait—" But it's too late. He's already enveloped in the crowd. Anna turns back to me. Her lips turn upward in an expression that I wouldn't quite call a smile. It's more of a nervous twitch, and it's over almost as soon as it's begun. "Well, he sure is ... confident," she says.

I lower my head, but keep my eyes aimed right at her. "You don't have to help out with the children's Christmas gift program if you don't want to. I'm sure Mr. Reed will be able to find someone else to fill the vacancy."

Anna jerks her head back. "I never said I didn't want to help. I just don't know if I can. I have a prior commitment to watch my niece on the evenings that my sister is at work. She works three days, then she's off for three, and I can never keep her schedule straight."

"So your hesitation has nothing to do with the fact that you don't want to be around me? Because—call me crazy—I kind of think that has a lot to do with it." Will she hold my Black Friday behavior against me forever?

"Well, you would be wrong about that, Mr. Hawkins."

"Please, call me Daniel."

She pauses. "I'd really prefer if we maintain a more professional affiliation with one another."

"Because I make you uncomfortable."

"Please, stop assuming you know how I feel." She looks down at her hands, which, I've noticed, she has been wringing for the last few minutes. "Besides, you don't make me uncomfortable. Not the least bit."

I don't believe her. She'll barely make eye contact with me, and she gets all fidgety and apprehensive when I'm around. I wish there was something more I could say to wipe away her objections to me, but I'm at a loss. I've already apologized about the TeddyTab incident, and I don't know if doing it again will make any difference. So instead, I prepare to make my exit. I take a few steps backward, then pause. "I hope you decide to help out with the program, Anna. I agree with what Mr. Reed said. I think you'd be an asset to the team."

Her big blue eyes stare into mine. "Thank you, Mr. Hawkins. I *will* think about it."

Well, at least that's something. A few seconds pass, and I realize she's still staring at me, like she has no idea what to say next. At a complete loss for words myself, I swallow, then hook my index finger around my suddenly tight shirt collar and give it a tug. "I'm sure we'll meet again soon," I say, like I jumped straight out of a 1940s black-and-white film. I feel like face-palming myself.

Anna opens her mouth to speak, but before she can say a word, a woman I don't recognize runs up to her and skids to a stop beside her. She's practically panting. "Anna, I've been looking all over the place for you." The woman is on the shorter side with dark hair. She grips Anna's forearm. "Grant Deluso is asking for you."

Anna turns to the woman, then looks back at me. "I'm sorry, Mr. Hawkins, but I'd better go."

I nod. "Yes, well, good luck with the auction. I need to get going myself." I offer her a small wave.

"Thank you. And ... have a good evening."

As I walk out the door, I think about the *better* impression I'd so badly wanted to make on Anna. It wasn't a huge improvement upon my first, but I do know one thing—my once-strong stance against dating again is growing weaker each time I see her. It's like the ice forming on Lily Lake just outside of town. It may look solid, but it won't hold any weight. Put one foot on it, and you're likely to fall right through.

And falling is what scares me the most.

# CHAPTER 12

# *Daniel*

I pull into my driveway at eight. After leaving the auction, I was far too agitated to go home, so I spent quite a while driving aimlessly around town, trying to make sense of the conflicting feelings I have about Anna. No matter how hard I try to shove them down, they keep popping back up.

When I first realized Anna was at the auction, I was filled with hope. Hope for a second chance to introduce myself, yes, but part of me wanted even more than that. And that's the part of myself that frustrates me, especially since whatever crazy feelings I have for this woman are clearly not reciprocated. My presence only seems to frazzle and overwhelm her. As much as I hate to admit it, it probably would be better for both of us if she turns down Alvin Reed's invitation to help with the children's gift program. Seeing her several days a week and feeling this attraction to her, all the while knowing she can't stand me—I don't think I'm up for that kind of rejection.

I open the front door to my house and find my brother-in-law sprawled out on the couch with one leg hung over the back and the other draped across the coffee table.

Sleeping like a baby.

I lean against the door until it clicks shut. Then I clear my throat. "Thanks for watching Madison again."

Kurt shoots up with a start. "No problem." He shakes all over like a dog stepping out of the lake after a swim, then wipes the side of his mouth with the back of his hand. "How was the auction?"

I shrug out of my sport jacket and toss it onto the recliner. "It was ... interesting." After loosening my tie, I head into the kitchen for a drink. When I return to the living room, Kurt hasn't budged.

He looks at me with one eyebrow raised. "Dude, I just spent the evening with a six-year-old. If I'm going to live vicariously through you, I'm gonna need a few more details."

Should I tell Kurt about the beautiful new art director who can't stand the sight of me? Probably not, considering the fact that he's my late wife's brother. That makes him the last person I want to confide in regarding my budding feelings for another woman. "It was an auction," I say. "There were photographs all over the room. Is that enough detail, or should I go on? And don't you need to get home? It's past your bedtime."

"I'm starting to get my second wind." Kurt swivels around, his feet hitting the carpeted floor with a thud. He presses his back against the couch and folds his hands behind his head. Looks like he plans to stay a while. "Tell me more about your night. I'm sure it was more exciting than mine."

Now he wants to chat? In the ten years we've been friends, Kurt has never once asked me about anything that doesn't have to do with food, sports, or fishing.

After unbuttoning the top button of my shirt, I lower myself into the recliner. "All right, since you're in such a talkative mood, I might as well indulge you—but don't complain if I bore you to tears." I breathe in deeply. "The auction I went to tonight was a fundraiser for the food bank's new distribution center."

"The one you're designing? So this was a work thing?"

"You could say that."

"Who else went to this auction? Anyone I would know?"

What's with the twenty questions all of a sudden? I grit my teeth and shake my head slightly. "I don't think so. Alvin Reed was there. He's the executive director of the food bank. I've worked with him on the design."

"Huh." His head bobs a few times. "I'm sure he's a great guy, but I was hoping for someone a little more exciting. Sounds like I'll have to do my vicarious living through someone else."

I shift uncomfortably in my seat. "Well, there was this woman there, too. She actually works at the art center, although I didn't know that until tonight."

Kurt leans forward. "Ah, now you've got my attention."

I flip my hand toward him. "There's really nothing more to say. We met yesterday morning. And again today at the mall."

"What's she like? She works at a gallery, so is she, you know, artsy-craftsy?" He wiggles his fingers in the air.

"I don't even know what that means." I try to picture Anna in my mind, her flawless skin, her full mouth, those blue eyes ... but Kurt doesn't need to know those details, or he might try to go after her himself. "She has long wavy hair, seems to like dangly jewelry."

"She sounds like a hippie."

"Sort of, but she's more of a classy hippy. She pulls it off well."

Kurt's brow arches up. "You like this girl."

Is that what this feeling is? *Like*? It feels more like torture. "I don't know. I think I'm starting to, but it all feels pretty foreign to me."

"It has been a while," he says with a knowing smile. "Did you ask her out?"

Snorting a laugh, I shake my head. "She would barely talk to me tonight. I'm pretty sure she hates me."

"You always chased the ones who played hard to get."

"Yeah, well, I'm afraid I'd be chasing this one for a long time." I work my jaw. "She made it clear she's not interested."

Kurt rubs his chin. "I have to say, I knew this day would eventually come, and I thought it would be much weirder to hear you talk about someone who wasn't my sister ... but it's really not that weird at all. Actually, I think it's time." He nods twice. "I think you should go for it. Make a fool of yourself. Ask this woman out. If she says no, then you can chalk it up to experience. At least you tried, right? But if she says yes, then ..." A mischievous twinkle reflects in his eyes.

I run both hands through my hair as I shake my head. "There is no way I'm asking this woman out. We didn't meet under the best circumstances, and I think she'd rather forget I exist."

"Huh. Well, maybe you're on the right track. That's how things started with my sister, and that worked out pretty well for you."

Yeah, after almost two years of going out of my way to get her attention.

Because I was the wide receiver for our college's football team, Leah had seen me as nothing more than her twin brother's jock friend and wasn't interested in the least. But, like with Anna, Leah made me feel things—things I'd never felt for anyone else, so I kept trying. Kept pursuing. I'd even enlisted Kurt to set his sister straight, to talk me up and mention my good points when I wasn't around. And somehow, it worked. When I finally got up the nerve to ask her out, she said yes.

Kurt rises from the couch, then yawns and stretches at the same time. "Well, you know how much I like a good heart-to-heart, but if you don't mind, I think I'll head home. That kid of yours wore me out."

I chuckle at the image of Kurt sprawled out on the rug like a mermaid or galloping around the living room, neighing like a horse. I've spent time with my daughter. I know what it's like.

I follow him as he saunters toward the door. "Thanks again for coming over," I say. "I'll see you tomorrow in church." Kurt turns the knob, but before he can leave, I place my hand on the trim board. "Hey, Kurt?"

He stops. "Yep?"

"Thanks for being cool with this. I doubt anything will come of it, but thanks for not judging me."

He looks down at his feet. "Leah would want you to be happy."

I scratch the back of my head and nod as Kurt steps outside and closes the door. I hope what he said is true. Leah wouldn't want Madison to be stuck with just me for the rest of her life. She's only six.

But am I really ready to start a relationship from ground zero with someone else? With all the frayed nerves and the second-guessing, it's almost easier to remain single. And at the age of twenty-nine with a little girl to think of, dating will be a whole new animal—and I'm almost a decade out of practice. Even if I thought I stood a chance, which I don't, how would I start trying to win Anna over? What so-called trick cards do I have in my hand? While I had Kurt to run interference between me and Leah back in college, there's no one to be my wingman this time. Anna doesn't know Kurt. Who would help me work my way into her good graces? We don't share any mutual friends, unless you count Alvin Reed, and I'm not counting him.

Shaking my head, I start for my bedroom, then stop. It's not entirely true that Anna and I don't have *any* mutual friends. We may not run in the same social circles, but we do share a mutual *acquaintance*, so to speak.

I continue down the hall, smiling. Looks like it might be time to enlist the help of my furry yet expensive friend—TeddyTab.

# CHAPTER 13

# Anna

The Sunday morning sun peeks through the inch-wide gap between the wall and my bedroom curtains, shining like a spotlight in my eyes and rousing me from my sleep in the middle of a pleasing, yet unsolicited dream. Daniel Hawkins, dressed in the same blue sport coat and tie as last night, had just asked me out for a romantic dinner. Dream Anna had said yes without hesitation. Flashing his perfect smile, Daniel had pulled me into his arms, lowered his head, closed his eyes—and that's when I woke up.

Now all I want to do is go back to sleep.

I pull my covers over my head and whisper-scream into the darkness. "No!" I can't purposefully think about Daniel Hawkins. That's the last thing I need. He's the reason I couldn't fall asleep last night. I spent hours tossing and turning, regretting how I'd been so standoffish around him. He'd asked me to call him Daniel, and what did I say? "I'd prefer to keep our affiliation professional—*Mr. Hawkins*." Ugh! Only an idiot would say something like that to a man like him. I wouldn't be surprised if he never speaks to me again.

I push my covers down and groan. I rarely let myself get this worked up over a guy. How has Daniel Hawkins burrowed so deep into my skin? I barely know him. And I still don't know for sure that he's not married. He has a child. So what's the story with the mother? There are so many unknowns there, I'm probably better off just forgetting about him.

If only I could.

Just as I drape my arm across my forehead, there's a knock on my bedroom door. I sit up and see Tamara poking her head into my room.

"Breakfast is ready."

I smile at her. "Thank you. Sorry I overslept." I won't mention the fact that I was trying to oversleep a little more and finish my dream. "I had planned on making pancakes this morning."

"I stopped in an hour ago, and you didn't budge. I thought I'd let you snooze a bit longer." Tamara slips into the room and sits on the edge of my bed. "You got home late last night. How'd the auction go?"

The bed springs creak as I scoot back to lean against my headboard. "It went pretty well."

"Pretty well?" The edges of her mouth turn down. "For how anxious you've been all week, I'd hoped it would go better than that."

"Oh, the auction itself went great. We raised a decent amount of money for the new distribution center."

"So what's with the sullen mood this morning?"

I sigh. Do I dare mention the fact that Daniel—Mr. Gorgeous from the mall, as Tamara calls him—had been at the auction? That his presence had thrown my world into a tailspin, causing me to lose my composure in front of dozens of people? And that despite my best efforts to deny the man's existence, I'd dreamt about him last night?

Probably not, unless I want Tamara to remind me how long it's been since I've been on a date. Choosing not to divulge my secrets, I say, "I don't know what my problem is." I swing my legs over the edge of the bed and stretch my arms above my head. "I'll get dressed and meet you in the kitchen in two minutes."

"Make it one minute. Kelsey can't wait much longer. I've already caught her snitching sausage links from the pan."

"I'll hurry." Once Tamara is out of the room, I rise from my bed and pull a cable-knit cardigan from my closet. After wrapping it around my T-shirt and flannel boxers, I pause and lift my head heavenward to pray.

"Heavenly Father, I don't understand what's gotten into me ever since meeting ... well, you know who. I've been having irrational feelings toward him, but I know my emotions can't be trusted. I know full well the heartache that trusting the wrong man brings, and I won't let that happen to me again. I need your strength to put Daniel Hawkins out of my mind—for good." I lower my head, say, "Amen," and then hurry to the kitchen to grab breakfast before I'm late for church.

As much as I hoped that God would speak directly to me during the church service yesterday, I have to admit that the sermon was no help whatsoever. All throughout the rest of the afternoon and evening, I struggled to quiet my pastor's words from Psalm 37:4 that played like an endless refrain in my head.

"Delight yourself in the Lord, and he will give you the desires of your heart."

It's my heart's desires that are the problem! Receiving them will only lead to more trouble. I really could've used some verses about changing one's heart, or squelching desires that will only lead to misery and anguish. Now that would've been an uplifting sermon.

But now it's Monday, and I'm ready to think about anything other than ... *he who shall remain nameless.* If I could just have one day without his gorgeous brown eyes invading my mental space, that would be amazing.

"Are we gonna stand here and stare into the void all day, or are we gonna move these ginormous boxes out of the way?"

I look up. Carla's eyebrows are lifted so high they've disappeared behind her bangs.

"I'm sorry, I must've been daydreaming." Again. "Just let me figure out the best way to do this."

"We probably shouldn't have told Chuck Allen he could just leave them *anywhere*." She uses her fingers to make quotes. "Next time, let's be more specific."

Carla's absolutely right, and had we known that this months' featured artist would drop off his pieces just inside the entry door, making it almost impossible for people to get in or out, we would've given more explicit instructions. But we didn't, because why would anyone leave a pile of super-heavy boxes in front of an entry door? But he did, and at this point there's nothing we can do about it other than figure out how to get them from here into the main gallery where they belong. I squint and angle my head to properly assess the situation.

Since November is drawing to a close, it's time to set up the "Season of Lights" exhibit that will run from December through January. Many of the featured pieces come from Chuck Allen, an artist from the North Shore who specializes in recycling old metal into star-shaped art. Unfortunately, we didn't realize how heavy many of the pieces would be. We typically don't ask the artists to assist with setup, but this time we should've made an exception.

Determined not to let these heavy packages get the best of me, I bend down and place my hands on either side of the one in front of me. "I think I'm ready now."

"Okay." Carla grabs the other side. "We'll lift on three. One, two, three—lift."

I groan through clenched teeth as I summon all the upper-body strength I possess. The box rises off the ground, but just barely.

Carla peers around the side of the box. "Are you sure you're not gonna drop it? These things could break a toe, you know."

"I'm about ninety-eight percent certain I *will* drop it. The question is when."

"Then let's set it down."

*Thank you, Lord.* I breathe a sigh of relief when the box is safely returned to the ground.

Hands on hips, Carla stares at the tall, brown carton and then back at me. "We only moved it about three inches."

I scratch my head. "I say we leave these here until someone stronger comes in."

Carla gestures over her shoulder. "Maybe I should get the dolly from the back room. That might make it easier."

"Wait, we have a dolly? Why didn't you mention that before?"

"I forgot about it until just now."

As Carla heads to the back room, I start peeling the packaging tape from the largest box so I can get a better look at these things. Just as I rip the long strip of tape free and start to ball it up in my fist, I notice a smaller, twelve-by-twelve square box that I hadn't seen before, sitting just to the side of the door.

Now this is the box we should've started with, not the heaviest and largest of the bunch. I abandon the job of tape-ripping and navigate through the Stonehenge-like maze of packages until I reach the smaller box. I bend down to pick it up, noting that it weighs practically nothing compared to the others. No way are its contents made of steel. Maybe this one isn't even from Chuck. I turn it over and over to examine each side. No tracking sticker or return address label. Only my name and the art center's address are written in black marker across the top.

What could this be? I'm not expecting any other shipments today.

Curiosity forces me to the back room, where I set the box on the counter and begin digging through drawers for a pair of scissors. I slit the clear packing tape down the middle and lift the outer flaps of the box.

Carla backs out of the storage closet, then wheels the dolly around to face me. "Whatcha got there?"

"I'm about to find out." I rip the paper away from the box. My breath catches when I see what's inside. "TeddyTab!" I pull the packaging materials out, searching for some kind of an invoice or note. Big Dealz must've gotten their backordered shipment early. But even so, they shouldn't have sent one to me. I haven't even paid for the bear yet. The rain check merely ensures that I'll get the sale price when the bear is back in stock. And how did they get my work address?

Unless ...

My hands still as realization hits me—this bear isn't from the store. There's only one person who could've sent it.

And here I thought I could go just one day without thinking about him.

# CHAPTER 14

# *Anna*

I finish putting the last of the clean supper dishes in the cupboard while Tamara helps Kelsey pick out something to watch on TV. I wait until Kelsey is completely enthralled with the dancing princesses on the screen before I clear my throat loudly, snagging Tamara's attention. Curling my index finger toward me, I beckon her to join me in the kitchen. "I have something to show you," I say in a loud whisper.

She tiptoes across the living room floor and stops right in front of me, hunkering down like we're on a secret mission. "What is it?" she asks, her hand cupped around her mouth.

"Follow me into the hallway. I don't want Kelsey to see."

With Tamara close behind, I sneak to the hall closet where I've hidden the box I received at work today. "Wait 'til you see what was delivered to the art center." Pushing several long winter coats out of the way, I reach toward the back of the closet and pull out the box, then turn and hold it out for Tamara to see.

She eyes it curiously, lifts the flaps, and peers inside. She gasps. "Are you kidding me? Where did you get this?"

Tamara's enthusiasm is so contagious, I have to stop myself from jumping up and down. "It showed up at work today. Someone dropped it off anonymously."

One of her eyebrows slowly rises. "*Someone?*" She continues to stare at me.

I place a hand to my chest. "I promise, I didn't see who it was, but I think we both know there's only one person who could've done it."

"Yes, the very handsome Mr. Daniel Hawkins." Tamara pulls the teddy's see-through package from the larger box and clutches it to her chest. "Have you decided how you're going to thank him?"

I scrunch my face at her. "What? No. I haven't given it any thought at all." Okay, so that's not exactly true, but Tamara does not need encouragement.

Tamara clucks her tongue at me. "You can't just take a two-hundred-dollar bear from the guy and give him nothing in return."

"I wasn't planning on giving him *nothing*," I say, offended that my sister would think so little of me. "I figured I'd pay him for it and give him my rain check when I see him Thursday night at the volunteer meeting." Yes, I've decided to help out with the children's gift program, regardless of whether Daniel Hawkins participates or not. It's the right thing to do.

Tamara stares at me with a gaping mouth. "Thursday night? You're going to let the poor man sit there for three days wondering whether or not you even got the bear? And if you did, whether you appreciated it or not? That's way too long. You need to go to his office tomorrow. Bring him the rain check and two hundred dollars cash, along with an invitation to join you for coffee sometime as a thank you. Or, better yet, dinner. No! Tell him you'll *make* him dinner." She winks at me.

My cheeks warm with embarrassment. "I am not asking him out, and I'm definitely not making him dinner." Besides, eating my food would probably send him running in the other direction. "But I can go to his office on my lunch break if you think it's that important. I have his business card somewhere." On my night-stand. Where I stare at it every night before bed.

Tamara rubs her hands together like she's trying to start a fire. "I wish it wouldn't be weird for me to go with you, because I would love to see the look on his face when you walk in."

"I bet you would," I say. "But there won't be anything to see, because he won't care whether or not I walk in. He'll probably just tell me to leave the money on his desk or give it to his assistant. I'm sure he only sent this bear to me because he still feels bad for how he ended up with it in the first place. It's a way for him to ease his guilty conscience. A peace offering, that's all. An olive branch, maybe."

Tamara's eyes narrow. "No. There's more to it. I think he likes you. I think he's using this bear as leverage so he can get what he really wants for Christmas this year—you!"

I reach for the biggest yet softest thing I can find in the hall closet, which turns out to be a spare pillow, and chuck it at my sister's head. "Now you've gone too far," I say in mock annoyance.

Laughing, she shakes the TeddyTab in my face. "Admit it— Daniel Hawkins is *not* a bad guy, and you like him."

I force the bear down and out of my sight. "I will admit no such thing." And I will definitely not admit the fact that my heart hasn't stopped racing since I agreed to stop by Daniel's office tomorrow.

CHAPTER 15

*Daniel*

This is not the relaxing evening I had planned. Today was stressful. I had a lot of meetings with people who were very hard to please. That's not unusual, but today just seemed worse. Because it's Monday night, I had planned on putting Madison to bed and catching the second half of the football game. I need to unwind, decompress. Not think about anything hard. But instead, I'm wearing an apron and standing in front of my open pantry, searching for chocolate chips.

This is not how I pictured my night going.

There was one bright spot in my crazy day, though, when I received the text from my brother-in-law late this morning, saying that the delivery to the art center went off without a hitch. When I read those words, I felt as though a weight had been lifted. At least *something* was moving in a positive direction.

Of course now I don't have a gift for Madison to open on Christmas morning. I may not have thought this whole thing through, but I still have time to figure things out on that front. Besides, Madison has not once mentioned wanting a TeddyTab, at least not to me. Maybe Kurt was wrong all along. Or maybe Madison likes the TeddyTab theme song more than the actual toy, which works for me, since the bear is way over my normal budget for a single Christmas gift. And if it helps smooth things over with Anna, then it's a win-win. I save money, Anna isn't so averse to spending time with me ... everything is right in the world.

Unfortunately, Kurt didn't actually see Anna when he made the delivery, and he wasn't able to stay long enough to see how she reacted when she opened the box. He just dropped and dashed. So in the spirit of optimism, I'm *assuming* she was overjoyed to have the TeddyTab in her possession. I even waited around my office for an extra hour after work, much to the annoyance of Madison's after-school babysitter, because I thought or hoped ... okay, I *expected* her to show up in my office with the bear in her arms and a huge smile on her face. It didn't happen, but it doesn't hurt to dream.

So I got home late, dinner was late, and now it's almost seven thirty on a school night. Madison should be getting ready for bed soon, and I should be watching football, but instead we're baking cookies.

Yes, cookies.

As soon as I picked up Madison from the sitter, she reminded me that it's officially the "Christmas season" and practically begged me to bake Christmas cookies with her. She was so excited about it. When she looked up at me with those big brown eyes, I couldn't say no—even though I'd had a rough day. I'm not about to let my little girl down. Leah would've loved making cookies with Madison, and I'm going to do my best to keep her Christmas traditions going strong.

Never having made cookies from scratch before, I'm not quite sure how to begin, which is why I've been staring into the pantry for the past five minutes. I scan up and down until my eyes catch sight of the chocolate chips. Perfect. I snatch the yellow-and-brown bag and toss it in the air, catching it in the cradle of my arm like the wide receiver I was in college.

I glance at the counter stool where Madison is seated, staring at me.

"I caught the chocolate chips, sweetie. Aren't you impressed?"

Her brow wrinkles. "We don't need chocolate chips. We're making cutout cookies, right, Daddy?"

"Um ... sure, princess. Cutout cookies sound perfect." But chocolate chip sounds even better than perfect. Why do Christmas cookies have to be different than regular cookies? Maybe we could whip up some chocolate chip cookie dough and cut it into Christmas shapes.

Joining Madison at the counter, I flip through the pages of Leah's cookbook until I find the sugar cookie recipe, then allow my eyes to scroll down the list of ingredients. I stop when I come to one that puzzles me. *Cream of tartar.* Do we have that in the kitchen somewhere? I know I've never used it before. If we do have it, it's probably pretty old.

More than likely, cream of tartar is a spice and not an actual cream, so it probably isn't in the refrigerator. I return to the pantry where I found the chocolate chips and fumble through the spice rack, knocking over small plastic cylindrical containers. Nutmeg, cloves, ginger ... no cream of tartar. Maybe it *is* in the refrigerator. I know I have tartar *sauce* in the refrigerator. That's a necessity, given that I'm an avid fisherman during both summer and winter. So maybe, if I don't have cream of tartar, I could substitute tartar sauce. They're both creamy and have the word *tartar* in them. How different can they be?

I pull the glass jar from the back of the refrigerator and examine it closely. The sight of dark green flecks of relish in the jar makes me wince, and I'm pretty sure Madison's reaction would be worse. I put the jar back and shut the refrigerator door. Maybe the cookies will taste better if I omit everything with tartar altogether.

The cookies took forever to bake. It would've been nice to know ahead of time that the dough had to chill for up to two hours before it could be rolled out and cut into shapes. When I read that in the recipe, my blood pressure spiked, so I took matters into my own hands—I stuck the bowl of dough in the freezer for twenty minutes. We ended up with a sticky mess all over the counter and the rolling pin. Madison didn't climb into bed until well after ten, and she has school tomorrow. She's going to be cranky.

*I'm* going to be cranky tomorrow. Heck, I'm already cranky.

After an entire evening spent baking cookies, I have to admit I've learned two things. First, someone needs to declare chocolate chip cookies the official Christmas cookie because the dough does not need to be cut into Christmas shapes. And second, I should've set aside way more than one hour of time for cookie baking.

Madison doesn't seem to mind the fact that our cookies turned out a little on the brown and crispy side, and the shapes aren't the least bit recognizable. She'll eat anything with sugar in it. Next time, though, I think I'll skip all the hassle and buy the premade dough that comes in those handy break-apart chunks.

And when I say *next time*, we're talking next Christmas. I am done with cookies for the season.

# CHAPTER 16

# *Anna*

There is no way I'm going to Daniel's office during my lunch break today.

Tomorrow is the first of December, which means our "Season of Lights" exhibit officially opens in less than twenty-four hours. We usually get a lot of visitors during the first few weeks of an exhibit, and since it's December, we also have to decorate the gallery and make it more festive. There is no way I can possibly leave—even for half an hour. It wouldn't be fair to Carla.

As if my thoughts have beckoned her, Carla walks through the front door carrying two boxes stacked on top of each other. They're from the print shop.

"Wait 'til you see these," she says as she heads toward the workroom, which isn't much more than a glorified closet off to the left of the main gallery.

Eager to see the newly printed flyers, I follow her into the small space. She plops the boxes onto the table, one beside the other, and then proceeds to remove their lids. One is full of promotional bookmarks and postcards, and the other contains full-color flyers describing each piece in the new exhibit.

I pull a postcard from the box nearest to me and hold it up, examining it. "These are beautiful. The printer did a fantastic job."

Carla nods. "So much better than our ancient copy machine."

"And so much faster," I add.

After replacing the lids on both boxes, Carla pauses, then looks up at the round clock on the wall above our heads. She turns to me. "Aren't you supposed to be somewhere?"

My heart thumps against the wall of my chest. Why did I have to go and tell Carla my plans? "Uh ... I had planned on *maybe* swinging by to see Daniel Hawkins, but with everything we have to do," I say, gesturing toward the gallery, "I don't think it's going to be possible."

Carla eyes me through narrowed lids. "Really? You think we're that busy?"

My cheeks grow hot under her scrutiny. "Yes. I'm feeling almost overwhelmed."

She tilts her head. "What exactly is it that's overwhelming you?"

"Honestly? The thought of stopping by Daniel's office." I grimace. "I don't know why I let Tamara talk me into this. Daniel is a busy man—a man who is at work right now. He doesn't need me stopping by and adding to his stress."

Carla folds her arms across her chest. "From what I witnessed at the auction, I have a feeling you would be a welcome distraction."

I roll my eyes. "You're almost as bad as Tamara."

"Why, because neither of us wants to see you waste a golden opportunity? I may have only met the man once, but that was enough to deduce that he is hot!" She does a little shoulder-shimmy when she says the word *hot*. "He's also a nice dresser, he has a good job, and he seems like a genuinely nice guy. What could possibly be holding you back?"

I scratch the back of my neck and turn my face downward. "I'm just ... not the best judge of character. I don't know his story. It could be complicated."

"Then ask him what his story is. Get to know him. If you think he comes with too much baggage, then you can bow out before you've gotten in too deep. Also, there's nothing wrong with just being friends with the guy. But you'll never be anything to him if you avoid him like he's got some contagious skin condition."

I laugh at the image her words conjure in my head. "Sometimes I think it'd be easier if he did have something like that. I've never felt such a strong pull toward a man I've only just met."

"Then you definitely need to find out what that's about!" Carla nearly shouts the words. She glances again at the time. "It's almost noon. Go. I can handle the immense workload until you return."

My pulse begins to race. Suddenly aware of the fact that I haven't taken a break all morning, I run my hands down the front of my shirt. "How do I look? Do I have pit stains? Am I too wrinkled? How's my hair?"

She smiles and gives me two thumbs up. "You look gorgeous. Now get going so I can eat my lunch. I packed a tuna sandwich today, assuming you'd be out for a while. You don't want to be here when I pull it out of my bag ... do you?"

My stomach revolts just thinking about the smell. "You know I don't."

Carla snickers, then heads toward the back room, leaving me alone with my nerves. The persistent pounding in my chest will only get worse the longer I stand here, so I head toward the front door, stopping by the desk to grab my purse and the envelope for Daniel, and walk out to my car.

As I drive the short distance to Daniel's building, conflicting thoughts clash in my brain. This could be a huge mistake, but it also might *not* be. Daniel could truly be a good guy. I know decent men exist, I've just never been lucky enough to attract one of them. But have I attracted Daniel? Could Tamara be right, that his giving up his TeddyTab was more than just a goodwill gesture? Today I might find out definitively where he stands—as long as I don't trip and fall flat on my face when crossing the threshold into his office.

Once I've reached the two-story brick building that matches the address on the business card, I pull up alongside the curb and take deep breaths until the beating of my heart slows to a normal, steady rhythm. I can do this. Maybe I've panicked and lost all sense when I've been around him before, but those times caught me by surprise. Today I am expecting to see him. I'm prepared.

I pull my coat tight against my chest as I walk through the doors and into the lobby. The large sign on the wall tells me that Daniel's office is on the second floor, so I take the steps to my left. When I reach the offices of Hawkins and Burke, I push open the glass door and am greeted by a woman with graying hair seated behind a large wooden desk.

"Can I help you?" she asks.

I clear my throat. "Yes, I'm here to see Daniel Hawkins. He's not expecting me, and I'm just now realizing I probably should've called first."

The woman smiles at me. "He's in a meeting. What is your name?"

"Anna McAllister."

She picks up the handset from the phone on her desk. "I can call the conference room and get a message to him that you're waiting."

"No!" I shout, pushing my hand out in front of me like a traffic cop. "I mean, that will not be necessary. I don't want to interrupt anything. It's not that important. I just have something to drop off for him, that's all."

"Oh, well you're welcome to leave it on his desk. His office is the first one on the right." She points to an open door a short distance down the hall.

Tightening my grip on the envelope in my hand, I nod my head toward her. "Thank you. I'll just leave it ... in there." I turn and follow the hall toward Daniel's darkened office.

Inside I see a standing desk, which is backlit by a large

window. There's a computer on it with two monitors and a few potted plants beside that. A jar of pens sits next to his office phone along with a black tape dispenser. Framed diplomas hang on the wall to the right.

I carefully slink over to the desk and set the envelope right on the computer keyboard where he is sure to see it. I start to back away, then second-guess my decision. That envelope has two hundred dollars in it. If Daniel can see it plainly when he walks into the room, then so can anybody else who happens to stop by. I reach across the desk and slide the envelope into the shadows between the two monitors. There. Now it won't be visible until someone is actually standing at the desk.

Feeling satisfied, I brush my hands together. Now that my task is complete, a sense of relief washes over me. Relief tampered by a bit of disappointment, if I'm being honest. Because Daniel was in a meeting, this exchange didn't go quite as I'd planned. I didn't hand him the envelope in person. He didn't sweep me up into his arms and twirl me around the room like I may have envisioned a time or two—or seventy. But this mission was still a success. Daniel and I are back on good terms. We're even. I have the TeddyTab, he has the money and the rain check, and I didn't even have to make a fool of myself in the process. I don't know why I was so nervous about today.

As I turn to walk out of the office, my gaze snags on a framed photo on top of a filing cabinet. Drawn by the smiling faces looking back at me, I walk closer to get a better look. It's a picture of a young family of three standing in front of a flowering lilac bush. The man is Daniel, that much is certain. Same short brown hair, same gorgeous eyes. His arm is wrapped around a beautiful woman with even darker hair, and a little girl—his daughter, I presume—is standing between them, beaming. The girl looks to be about three or four in the picture. And the woman ... she's stunning. Smiling and happy, with a twinkle in her eye that was undoubtedly put there by Daniel himself. This is not a picture of an unhappy couple on the verge of breaking up. The woman in this picture would never walk out on Daniel, not if he can make her smile like that.

And he'd have to be a crazy person to leave someone like her, so maybe he didn't. Maybe he *is* married. He never said he wasn't. It was all Tamara—and Carla!—filling my head with silly ideas and crazy romantic notions. And yeah, I may have had a bodily, heart-stopping response to Daniel when I first met him, but if he's married, then none of that matters. My feelings don't matter. In fact, they've been totally inappropriate, and it all ends now. Right this second.

"Anna?"

At the sound of my name, I whip around. As I do, my hand crashes into the jar of pens on the desk, sending them flying. My face instantly flames with heat. "Daniel," I say as I reach across his desk, trying to collect as many pens as I can. "I was just ... I thought I would ..."

He hurries over to help me, bending to pick up several pens from the floor. "Please, don't worry about it," he says. "I can get them later." He straightens to his full height, sets the few pens he's collected on the desk, then slides his hands into his pockets. Beneath his rumpled brow, his eyes peer down at me. "I didn't know you were here. I would've ducked out of my meeting." Then his eyes brighten. "Actually, since we're alone, there's something I've been meaning to ask you—"

"No. Please—don't." I wave my hands in front of me. "I only came to give you this." I reach across the desk and grab the envelope, then hand it to him. "It's the money to repay you for the TeddyTab—which, by the way, you did *not* need to give me, but since you did, I will accept it with gratitude on behalf of my niece." I start backing toward the door. I need to go before I make an even bigger fool of myself. I waggle a finger in his general direction. "The rain check is also in the envelope so you can get your daughter a TeddyTab after Christmas, if you want to. But that's none of my business, so just ... do what you want with it." I've managed to reach the doorway, even walking backwards, which is a pretty impressive accomplishment. "Have a good afternoon, Mr. Hawkins." I turn around and immediately collide with the wall *next* to the door.

Okay, so I may have jumped the gun on praising my backwards walking skills. I rub my stinging forehead and nose, take one step to my right, then dash out of Daniel's office. I don't turn to look behind me as I speed walk down the short hallway, out the door, and down the staircase. I'm sure Daniel is smart enough not to chase after me, since he'd have to pass by his assistant's desk on his way out, and she knows he's married. It would *not* be a good look for him.

I exit the main lobby and step outside into the icy wind, but the air feels good on my flushed face. When I finally reach my car, I slip inside, slam the door, and rest my head against the cold steering wheel. I feel like an idiot. I would give anything to erase this day from my memory, make it like it never happened.

But it did. And I won't soon forget it.

I should never have come.

# CHAPTER 17

# Daniel

Immediately after Anna fled my office—for reasons I would love to know but have yet to figure out—I was bombarded with phone calls followed by back-to-back virtual meetings, and now I'm on my way to a site visit. If I didn't have so many commitments today, I would be at the Suomi Art Center right now, trying to figure out what had gotten Anna so unnerved. She'd left in such a hurry, I didn't even have a chance to offer her an ice pack for her face. That head-on collision with the wall must've hurt.

And that begs the question—why was she in such a hurry to escape? And what had distracted her so much that she'd run into a wall? Clearly something was bothering her. I only wish I had time to figure it out right now.

I pull my coat from the back of my chair and exit my office, closing the door behind me. As I pass by Lois's desk, I stop, open my mouth to ask her if she noticed anything strange about Anna's visit, then immediately press my lips together and shake my head. Lois looks up at me, her browns knit together in concern, and I frown.

"Do you ... need something, Daniel?" she asks.

Ah, dear Lois. Always so perceptive. I wave my hand through

the air, shooing away my unasked question as if it were a pesky fly. "Never mind, it's nothing. I'm on my way to South Elementary. They're considering adding another wing, and we're going to look at location options."

"Sounds good. I'll see you when you get back." She turns back to her computer and resumes her work.

I take two steps toward the door, then stop again. "Um, Lois?"

Her eyes slant upward as she smiles. "Yes?"

"Let me know if I miss any calls. Or ... if anyone stops by."

"I always do."

"That's right." I bob my head. It's in Lois's job description to do those things. She doesn't exactly need reminding. She's worked in this office longer than I have.

Lois rolls her chair away from her desk and takes off her glasses, then folds her arms across her chest and peers up at me. "Would you like to talk about what's bothering you, Daniel?"

I jerk my head back. "What do you mean? Nothing's bothering me."

She laughs, and the creases framing her eyes deepen. "I've known you for eight years now, ever since you became part of the Burke family, and eventually, this firm. I've seen you work through some pretty tough times, and even though you put up a good front, I can always tell when you're not okay."

I turn my head to the side and run a hand through my hair. I can't hide anything from Lois—not that I've made a huge effort to do so. She's practically part of the family. Leah's family. Before I joined this company, it was known as Burke Design Co., Burke being my father-in-law, Joseph Burke. After I finished my degree, Leah and I moved back here to her hometown of Lake Valley so I could start working with her dad. It's just me in the office now, since Joe and his wife, Bev, spend half the year in Tucson, but his name is still attached to the company and probably always will be. As long as he's breathing, he'll take on one or two small projects a year, just to stay busy. Lois has been his executive assistant for over two decades, and now she's mine. She isn't wrong when she says she knows me. She's been here through the good and the bad.

She eyes me through narrowed lids. "I hope you don't mind if I make an observation," she says.

"Go ahead."

"You seemed fine this morning, but ever since that woman—Anna, I think her name was—stopped by, you've been a bit … off."

I look up at the ceiling, then down at my feet. Anywhere but at Lois. "That might have something to do with it," I mumble while scratching my neck.

"Listen to me, Daniel." Although her words are commanding, her voice is soft and full of compassion. "I know it's none of my business, but I'm more than happy to help if I can, even if it's just to provide a listening ear."

I let my shoulders fall as I sigh, then I sink into the chair across from her desk. "I'm out of my depth here. There is something about that woman that makes her very hard to ignore, and believe me, I've been trying." I shake my head. "It's no use."

Lois leans forward, placing her hands on her knees. "That's not a bad thing, Daniel. You're allowed to have feelings for someone. There's no right or wrong amount of time that needs to pass before it's considered okay. When it comes to grief, loss, and moving on, there are no rules. It's different for everyone. Personally, I'm happy that you've met someone."

I stifle the urge to laugh out loud. "Yeah, well, I've met her, that much is true. Beyond that, I haven't made a lot of progress. I don't think my interest in her is reciprocated."

"Hmm." Lois hums, her lips pressed firmly together. "That wasn't the impression I got, at least not when she first arrived."

"What do you mean?"

She tilts her head to one side, then the other. "Well, she seemed very nervous at the prospect of seeing you today, and believe me, that is not how a woman acts when she's about to see someone she doesn't like. In fact, I doubt she would've stopped by at all if she didn't want to see you."

"Interesting."

Lois nods. "But then she left in such a hurry, and her demeanor had completely changed."

"That's the part that has me stumped," I say.

"Do you know what I would do?" Lois asks.

"No, but I hope you tell me."

That earns a smile from her. "I would pray about it. I know that sounds trite, but God knows what's going on inside that woman's heart and yours. He has a plan, and maybe it involves the two of you being together ... but maybe it doesn't. There's no sense in forging ahead and getting your heart tangled up with someone that isn't God's best for you in the first place."

"That's a good point," I say. "I have to admit I haven't exactly pursued God's leading in this situation. I wasn't expecting it. She —Anna—caught me by surprise."

"Sometimes the best things that happen to us are unplanned." Lois pulls her chair back toward her desk and replaces her glasses. "I'll be praying for you. Let me know if you ever need to talk again. I'm always here."

"I'll do that."

In this moment I am supremely thankful for all the people God has placed in my life—in both my family and my workplace. Lois is not only my administrative assistant, she's also like my favorite aunt. And since I have four biological aunts, that's saying a lot. Her advice is always spot-on, and this time is no exception. I need to give this situation over to the Lord. I may have prayed that he would help me make a good impression on Anna, but have I really asked if this is the direction I should be going, pursuing someone new? Am I truly seeking God's will for me, or am I making plans and asking him to join in them after the fact?

I may have no more answers than before, but I feel much better about the situation after talking to Lois. I rise from my seat and tap my finger twice against her desk. "Thanks for listening and for the advice. I know it's not part of the job."

"No worries," she says with a wink. "This conversation was off the clock."

*Anna*

I arrive home Tuesday evening a little after five. Tamara doesn't work until seven, so she's home with Kelsey. The minute I click the front door shut, Tamara shoots out of the kitchen, then sprints into the living room to meet me. Her eyes are wide and expectant. "So? How did it go? What did he say? I texted you like ten times, but you didn't reply."

I drop my tote bag beside the rocking chair that used to be our mother's and continue into the kitchen without saying a word. Tamara follows on my heels as I flip the switch on the electric kettle to make a cup of tea.

When I finally turn around to face my sister, her arms are folded across her chest. When her eyes meet mine, she does a double take. "What happened to your face?"

I shake my head. "I ran into a wall. But I'm fine. Carla had me ice it all afternoon."

She studies me for a beat. "Um, okay, but ... what about Daniel?"

Leaning back against the countertop, I sigh. "He's married. Just like I thought, like I tried to tell you and Carla, he's married. He has a beautiful wife, an adorable little girl, and I am never going to look at him or think about him again. I feel like a terrible person."

Tamara's shoulders sag. "I'm sorry, Anna. I was so sure about his feelings. He was giving off a vibe, you know? At the mall, when he looked at you ... he seemed really interested. And then he gave you his bear—"

I swipe my hand through the air, cutting her off. "If he's married and giving off a vibe, then he's someone I want to steer clear of."

Tamara frowns. "I can't believe I misread him."

I can, because Tamara is as bad as I am at judging people's true character—specifically *men's* true character. "We were both fooled," I say. "And because of that I'm not going to the meeting on Thursday night, so I can handle getting Kelsey to and from dance practice. I'm sure there are plenty of people who can fill that vacancy for Mr. Reed. Maybe Daniel's *wife* can help him out with the gift program."

Tamara grabs my hand and gives it a gentle squeeze. "This is my fault. I encouraged you to go to his office, and I put you in an awkward position. And now you're not going to the meeting? I thought that gift program would've been a great way for you to get involved in the community again."

I shrug. "It would've been, but it's okay. There are other ways to get involved that won't force me to be in the same room as the *married* man that I've been crushing on. Maybe I'll volunteer somewhere else. Maybe the food bank—as long as Daniel isn't also volunteering there." If he is, I'll try somewhere else. I will make sure that we never have a reason to cross paths on purpose again.

# CHAPTER 18

# *Anna*

Thursday evening, I drive Kelsey to her practice at the performing arts center, which is an extension of our town's senior high school. Tamara doesn't start work until seven, and normally she takes Kelsey to practice, and I pick her up. But tonight I told Tamara to stay home and relax before heading to work. If I drive Kelsey in, I'll have a legitimate excuse for missing the meeting tonight.

I really should be there, because I'm sure Alvin Reed was counting on me ... but I just can't do it. I'm not ready to be in a room with Daniel after what I found out. I'm still too upset to behave normally. Or maybe I'm just too embarrassed. Maybe he wasn't sending out any signals, and Tamara, Carla and I were simply hoping to pick up on something that wasn't actually there. Maybe he really has done nothing wrong. But I let my heart get carried away along with my imagination—which I promised myself I would never do again—and now I'm in recovery mode. I need time to regroup.

So now I'm sitting in the lobby of the performing arts center, trying to stay occupied for the duration of Kelsey's one-hour class. After about thirty minutes of scrolling through meaningless social media posts on my phone, I decide to get up and walk, get my blood flowing. I meander down the hall, taking in the student art displays that line the walls just like they did when I was in school here.

Not a whole lot has changed since then except the carpeting and the overhead light fixtures.

I pass the last framed painting and round the corner, then head up a few steps toward the auditorium doors. I used to spend hours here in high school, working on set design for each and every play and musical the student body put on, which was at least two a year. I lived for those days. Bringing fictional worlds to life through painted backdrops and custom-designed props was what inspired me to study art in college. This is where I realized my true passion.

I approach the double doors to the auditorium and consider going inside, just for old times' sake, when something on the wall catches my eye and stops me cold.

The auditorium has been renamed. When I was a student here, there was simply a generic plastic plate that read "auditorium" tacked up on the wall beside the door. Now there's a shiny bronze plate below a framed picture, and etched into the bronze plate are the words *The Leah Burke Hawkins Auditorium.*

Hawkins. Could it be?

One look at the picture above the name is all I need to confirm my suspicions. I know this woman's face. It's the same face from the picture in Daniel's office. This woman is Leah Burke, who later became Leah Hawkins, as in Mrs. Daniel Hawkins. Daniel Hawkins of Hawkins and Burke Architecture and Design, a company I now realize he co-owns with his father-in-law.

I shake my head in disbelief, even though I'm starting to remember more details, and I know I'm not wrong—I just don't want to believe it.

I may not have known Leah personally, but we grew up in the same town, went to the same school. She was three or four years ahead of me. I don't even know if we ever crossed paths, but I know her story. I remember when it all happened. After graduating from college, Leah worked in this very building as the high school choir director for only a few years when her life was tragically cut short—an aneurism, I believe. It was all over social media a couple of years ago. She left behind a little girl and a loving husband, and that husband was Daniel. How could I have missed the connection?

As the facts fall into place and the story takes shape, it suddenly becomes clear that I have made a terrible misjudgment. Without prompting, every single interaction I've had with Daniel plays through my mind like a highlight reel of bad behavior. I feel like the worst kind of person. Because of my insecurities and scars from past hurt, I wasn't kind to a man who did nothing wrong, a man who has already experienced enough pain to last a lifetime.

This is an excellent lesson on why a person should never form opinions about someone else without knowing the whole story. Too bad the lesson has come at a cost. I may have already burned every bridge that can get me back into Daniel's good graces. But I have to at least try, and I have to do it as soon as possible. If I could just make it to city hall before the meeting ends, maybe Daniel will still be there.

I look at my phone. Kelsey's practice ends in fifteen minutes, but so might the meeting. There's no time to go to city hall and be back here by seven, so I'll have to wait until Kelsey is done before I can leave, and I'll have to bring her with me.

My only hope is that Alvin Reed has a *lot* to discuss at the meeting.

No, that's not my only hope. I also hope that Daniel has a huge capacity to forgive, and that if he gives me another chance to get to know him, I won't blow it this time around.

*Daniel*

It's just after seven o'clock, and the meeting is wrapping up. Normally, I'd be thrilled. I prefer to keep meetings to an hour or less, especially when there isn't that much on the agenda. But tonight, I'm praying Alvin Reed goes off on some wild tangent. That's what he does whenever we meet at my office, so why can't he do that now? Anna hasn't shown up yet. I do recall her mentioning something about a dance rehearsal or something, but I keep hoping that any minute now, the door to this conference room will swing open, and she'll breeze in, apologize for being late, and take the seat beside me that I haven't allowed anyone else to occupy, even though several people have tried.

After talking to Lois the other day, I did spend some time in prayer over this situation with Anna. I gave my future—and any future romantic relationships—over to the Lord. I've done this countless times before with other things, but it seems I often have to do it again. And again. Submission is hard. Letting go doesn't come naturally to me. I'm a doer, a fixer. I solve problems. I work around obstacles. Handing over my developing feelings for Anna and giving them to the Lord is scary, but it's really the only option. Who knows what my future holds other than God? No one—certainly not me.

So as I sit here, glancing at the door for what must be the hundredth time, I take a deep breath and remember that it's in God's hands. Anna may still show up, but she also might not. If she doesn't, I might cross paths with her another day. Or not. She may be the one for me, or maybe God has someone else in mind. Or maybe he plans for me to remain single and to raise Madison on my own for the next twelve years.

*Please, Lord, don't let that be your plan.*

Alvin Reed claps his big hands together, startling me back to reality. "Well, I think I've taken up enough of your time," he says with a hearty chuckle. "I'll let you folks get home to your families."

"Wait!" I shout at the same time that my hand shoots up, like I'm in middle school and I know the answer to a really hard math question. "Did you mention where we're supposed to put the gifts once we've collected them?"

Alvin's eyes slant in my direction. "I believe I did, but if anyone is still unclear, we've set up a drop-off location in one of the old Sunday school classrooms on the lower level of St. Margaret's Church. We can store the items there until distribution day, since there's no available space for them at the food bank. The lower-level doors of St. Margaret's are always locked, so when you arrive, just go upstairs to the homeless shelter entrance and someone should be able to let you in." He smiles, gathers his papers together, and then stops, holding up his index finger. "Oh, that reminds me. There's one more thing I wanted to mention."

*Thank you, Lord,* I breathe in silent prayer.

"Over at the food bank we're in desperate need of help, as volunteers drop like flies during the holiday season. Everyone is busy, and we understand that, but if you'd like to consider gathering some folks from your workplace and signing up for a two- or three-hour shift packing boxes, that would be much appreciated. The sign-up is on our website."

Several people around the table nod their heads while murmuring their plans to help out at the food bank. Then, one by one, they each stand and push in their chairs before making their way to the exit. Guess that means this meeting is officially over. I hang back, waiting until every last person has left the room—even Alvin Reed—before walking slowly to the door.

Alvin stops in the doorway and turns to me. "I had hoped that Miss McAllister would come tonight. Because she didn't, I'm not sure if she plans on helping with the gift collection. Can you handle it on your own, or would you like me to find someone else to assist you?"

I shake my head. "I've got it. My brother-in-law is always around if there are too many donations to haul in one truck."

A throat clears from somewhere behind Alvin. "That won't be necessary. I can help."

At the sound of the familiar voice, my heart somersaults in my chest. I crane my neck to look beyond Alvin's wide shoulders and lock eyes with Anna, and in that moment I know.

Something has changed. I don't know what it is, but I have a very good feeling I'm about to find out.

# CHAPTER 19

# Daniel

I stare at Anna and she stares back. Neither of us says a word.

Alvin brushes his hands together. "Well, Daniel, I hope you can fill Anna in on what we discussed tonight. I'd better be getting home. My wife is holding supper for me, and I don't want to keep her waiting too long. You two have a good evening." He nods at each of us as Anna steps aside to let him through the doorway.

As he saunters down the hall, I notice a young girl seated in a chair just a few feet away. It's the girl from the mall, the one with the book who wasn't looking where she was going. "I see you brought a friend," I say.

Anna smiles as she looks over her shoulder. "Yes, my niece. She just finished up dance practice."

"I remember you mentioning that at the auction. That's why you couldn't make the meeting?"

She looks down at her hands, where I notice she's rubbing her palm with the opposite thumb. "Not exactly. I could've come late and left early. There was another reason that I stayed away."

When her gaze returns to mine, I can sense hesitation in her expression. There's an uncertainty there, and I wish I could wipe it away. "You don't owe me an explanation," I tell her.

"Actually, I do ... for my behavior toward you this past week." A blush covers her cheeks as she shrugs. "I haven't been the friendliest person."

I widen my eyes in mock surprise. "Really? I hadn't noticed."

She laughs, but the sound is more sad than happy. "Seriously, Daniel. I'd like to explain myself, but ... to be honest, it's a little embarrassing."

I wedge my foot against the wall for support as I lean against it. "I promise I won't laugh."

"It might be easier for both of us if you do." She rubs her forehead. "Okay, here goes." She winces, and the words tumble out of her mouth. "I thought you were married."

At that, I'm struck mute. I'm not quite sure how to respond. My first instinct is to blurt out that I am. I *am* married. Even after almost two years, it still stings to say anything other than those words. But I can't say them, because they're not true, not anymore. And I can't seem to form the words to say otherwise, because my mouth is no longer functioning. It's like my tongue has been tied up by tiny, invisible bandits, and it refuses to cooperate.

So I simply take a slow, deep breath, and shake my head while letting it out.

Anna lowers her gaze to the floor. "I know the truth now. Tonight during dance practice I walked by the auditorium, and that's when I saw your wife's picture. I recognized her instantly. She had almost the same expression as in the framed photo in your office."

The framed—ah. Now the episode from the other day is starting to make a lot more sense. The pens scattering across the desk, the hurried escape—Anna saw Leah's picture and panicked.

When Anna looks back up at me, her eyes are glistening. "I'm so sorry, Daniel, and not only for what you've been through, but for assuming things about you without knowing all the facts. It's just that when we met outside BigDealz on Black Friday, you said you were shopping for your daughter, so I thought you might be married. But then both my coworker and my sister assured me that you weren't, because of the vibe you were giving off."

"Wait," I say, jerking my head back. "I give off a vibe?"

She grimaces, and the skin around her eyes creases. "Um ... forget I said that part. I probably should've kept it to myself."

I wave my hand through the air between us. "No way, it's too late. You said it, so now you have to explain. What kind of vibe was I giving off? Was it creepy? Like a stalker vibe?"

Tilting her head back, she laughs, and the heaviness from a few moments ago melts away. "No, it was nothing like that. It was more ... you know, the kind of vibe that says maybe you want to spend more time getting to know someone."

"Huh." I had no idea my feelings were so obvious—not that I had put a ton of effort into hiding them.

Anna blinks up at me. "So is that an accurate interpretation? Or are my sister and Carla way off base?"

I take a minute to ponder that question. The fact that Anna just asked it and is still standing here and not running for the door is a really good sign. This is definitely not the Anna from my office on Tuesday, who collided with a wall trying to get away from me. And it's not the Anna from the auction, who tried to keep things strictly business and wouldn't even say my first name by itself. And it's *definitely* not the Anna from BigDealz. That Anna had a little temper.

Unlike all the other versions of herself that she's shown me so far, I think *this* Anna, the one right in front of me, just might be agreeable to getting to know me better. We've finally cleared up any and all misconceptions that have been keeping us at odds. Now all I have to do is overcome the intense anxiety that twists my stomach in knots every time I think about making some sort of move.

Expelling a quick breath, I run a hand through my hair, then shove it against the wall behind my back. "Okay, so either I'm not playing it as cool as I thought I was, or your sister and your friend are very perceptive." I shrug. "Either way, they're pretty spot-on. I would like to get to know you better. I've thought about you a lot since meeting you last Friday, and that hasn't happened to me in a long time. I just—I don't know how to do this, get to know you. I have a daughter. I also probably have more emotional baggage than some of the other guys out there. I may not be someone that *you* would be interested in getting to know. But even with all of that on the table, I'm still finding it hard to get you out of my head."

A deep red hue covers Anna's cheeks. She twists a piece of blond hair around her finger. "I don't think I want to be out of your head."

I wasn't prepared for that. "You don't?"

"No. In those in-between moments when I *didn't* think you were married, I was very interested in finding out more about you. So if you want to, maybe, spend some time together, I would definitely be okay with that."

My heart rate accelerates. "That's a relief." Only now I'm more nervous than ever. "There's no pressure, obviously. We would just be two friends hanging out."

"Friends," she repeats. "I think I like that better than two adversaries fighting over the same—" She stops suddenly, then looks over her shoulder at her niece before turning back to me. "The same toy," she whispers.

"We were never adversaries," I say. "I'm sorry if I made you feel that way. And I'm also sorry I didn't tell you about Leah, but it's just not something I mention when I introduce myself to people. But then again, it never seems like a good time to bring it up without things getting awkward. I don't want people feeling sorry for me the second they meet me."

She offers me a sad smile. "I can understand that better than I'd like to. I lost both of my parents in a single car accident. You should see the looks on people's faces when I tell them." Her eyes meet mine, and her brow rises. "It's very similar to the look you're giving me right now."

I lower my head and chuckle. "I'm sorry. It's a natural reaction, I guess. No one knows how to handle hearing something tragic like that, even if they've been through a tragedy themselves."

For a moment, neither of us says a word. The silence hangs in the air between us like a dense fog. I have to break the tension, so I opt for a swift subject change. I stand straighter and clear my throat. "Um, yeah, so ... about the gift collection thing. In the meeting, we talked about me possibly picking up the donations on Saturday and delivering them to St. Margaret's for safekeeping. Would you be interested in helping me? You know, since we're friends now."

Anna's lips curve into a smile. "I would love to help you on Saturday. My sister is off that day, so I'm totally free."

I exhale in relief. "Perfect. I'm looking forward to it."

After we exchange numbers and agree when and where to meet, she turns to her niece and lightly taps her on the top of the head. "Kelsey, it's time to go. It's a school night, so we should head home."

The girl closes her book and stands, and the three of us walk down the hallway toward the exit.

Once we're outside, I notice Anna's black sedan right away. It's parked close to my truck. In fact, ours are the only two vehicles left in the city hall parking lot.

Anna loads her niece into the back seat, buckles her up, and then closes the door. Then she turns to me. "I hope you plan on bringing your daughter on Saturday. I would love to meet her." Abruptly her eyes flash with alarm. "I mean, if you'd be okay with that. Otherwise, I totally understand if you don't like introducing her to your ... friends."

With my smile, I try to convey that I would like nothing more than to introduce Anna to Madison. Honestly, I'm having a hard time keeping my smile from overtaking my entire face. I take a few backwards steps toward my truck. "I'll bring Madison. I'm sure she'd love to play Santa's helper for the afternoon."

"Wonderful." Anna opens her driver's side door. "I guess I'll see you then."

I give her a wave and wait until she's safely out of the parking lot before starting my truck. As it warms up, I thank God for making things clear and for guiding my steps at this stage in the game. It's early yet, and I realize that. I'm trying hard not to get ahead of myself, but my feelings seem to have a mind of their own.

Speaking of feelings, I now have to go back to my house, where my brother-in-law is waiting for me to release him from his childcare duties. I only hope that during the ten-minute drive from here to there, I can figure out how to temper my excitement so Kurt doesn't ask me why I'm acting like a giddy school boy.

# CHAPTER 20

## *Anna*

"It looks like someone handed out jars of glitter to a bunch of five-year-olds and let them loose in here." Carla shakes her head as she sashays around me, broom in hand, sweeping up all of the glitter that has fallen to the ground. We've just finished setting up a Christmas tree in the center of the main gallery, and, despite the mess, it's a work of art. In fact, it's decorated with dozens of works of art. Each glittery ball dangling from the branches was made by a child from a local preschool who came to the art center for an ornament-making session earlier in the week, taught by our education assistant, Laura. If the kids come to the gallery before Christmas, they can take their ornaments home. For now, they're doing a good job of dropping glitter everywhere.

Apparently, little kids can never have enough glitter.

While we were decorating the tree, I filled Carla in on what I discovered at the auditorium during Kelsey's dance practice, and how I totally misinterpreted every single word Daniel has ever said to me, as well as his generous act of giving me his TeddyTab—which I kind of feel guilty for having, now that I know he's a single dad just trying to give his daughter the perfect Christmas gift.

"So, when are you going to see him again?" Carla asks.

I lean against the wall, arms crossed, watching her sway back and forth with her broom. "Tomorrow. We're collecting donations for the children's gift program."

"Too bad you can't find a reason to invite him here today."

"While I'm working?" I wrinkle my brow. "I wouldn't be able to get anything done. I'd be so nervous, I'd probably start knocking things over."

"Yeah, I can see how he would be very distracting. Personally, I could stare at him all day—and I suppose you could, too." She starts to chuckle, then places her hand over her mouth to stifle it. "Just like that time when you were up at the podium, trying to recall the name of our featured photographer and completely shut down. Remember? That was because of Daniel."

I roll my eyes at her. "I'm well aware." Especially since it was less than a week ago.

"I was so uncomfortable for you, just standing up there like a deer in headlights," Carla says. "I even went home that night and wrote about it in my journal."

"Please tell me that's not true," I say with a groan.

"Oh, it's true. That was a near catastrophe. But you pulled through like a champ." She play-punches my upper arm. "So, yeah, better not invite him to come here. He's too good-looking for his own good." Carla shakes her head at me, then bends down to sweep her glitter pile into the dustpan.

At four fifty-five, I'm about to lock up and head home for the day when my phone alerts me of an incoming text message. I pull it from my pocket and tap the screen. It's from Tamara.

**Heard some interesting news today. Not sure how to feel or what to tell Kelsey. You'll be home soon?**

Uh oh. This doesn't sound good. I assume this news involves Wayne, since Tamara mentioned Kelsey. I quickly type back a reply.

**Be home in 15. Please boil some water. Sounds like warm beverages are in order.**

I drive home in the dark, the sun having set about half an hour ago. The first thing I notice when I pull up to the house is the colorful lights twinkling through the living room window. Tamara and Kelsey must've been decorating.

I walk in the door and immediately my sister is in my space. Her hands are clasped in front of her and on her face is an apologetic grimace.

"I'm so sorry we started without you," she says. "Kelsey got home from school and couldn't wait to start decorating. I got a little tired of the begging, so I pulled the tree box down from the attic. I only meant to set up the tree and nothing else, but somehow Kelsey convinced me that stringing up the lights doesn't count as decorating."

I snicker as I drop my bag to the floor and kick off my shoes. "She's right—it's merely prep work."

Kelsey bursts into the room from the hallway. "Auntie Anna, you're home! Now we can do the ornaments."

Tamara holds up her hand. "Slow down there, little girl. Let your aunt settle in for a moment or two. We're going to have some tea, and then, when we're done, we'll start ... or finish ... decorating."

Kelsey gallops around the living room, holding invisible reins in her fisted hands, and then disappears down the hall.

Tamara shakes her head. "I would pay good money for that kind of energy. Especially working twelve-hour night shifts."

I nod. "Wouldn't we all?"

I take a seat at the dining table while Tamara fetches two mugs. The ceramic tea pot is already in the center of the table, as well as the sugar bowl and an assortment of tea bags. "This is just how Mom used to set it up," I say as I pour hot water into my mug. "I miss the tea parties we used to have with her."

"I do too," Tamara says. "I'm glad you'll still indulge me,

because Kelsey's not interested. If I serve hot chocolate instead of tea, then she'll sit with me for a few minutes."

I snicker. "Kids today don't have the patience for tea." We sip in silence for a few moments, and then, once I've checked the room for the presence of little listening ears, I set down my mug. "So what is this news you got today?"

Tamara takes one last sip before resting her mug on the table. She wraps both hands around it for warmth. "A coworker of mine has an old college friend who lives in North Dakota. Recently, this friend of hers started seeing someone who works for the pipeline."

"Wayne," I say without missing a beat.

Tamara nods. "Unfortunately, there's more. This woman has a little boy, and apparently, Wayne has moved in with them. They're like ... a family."

I stare at Tamara for a long moment while attempting to pull up my slackened lower jaw. "I guess it wasn't *only* work that was keeping him in North Dakota."

"Clearly, no. Now, this isn't anything that Kelsey needs to know," Tamara says. "She'd be heartbroken to find out that her dad—who hasn't bothered to call or text her in weeks—is living in a house with a little boy about her age. I mean, if he doesn't want to be a father, why is he acting like one to someone else's child when he has a daughter of his own who he completely ignores?"

I place a hand on her knee. "I'm sorry this is happening. I wish I knew what to do."

Tamara sighs, long and slow. "Me too. I can't say I'm surprised, though. He's never been the father that Kelsey needs. I've prayed about this for so long. I've given it over to the Lord, and I finally felt at peace, knowing that no matter what Wayne does or doesn't do, Kelsey has a heavenly Father she can trust who will never let her down. But now this happens, and it just stirs up all the old hurt I thought I'd dealt with. I mean, he's okay with having a little responsibility and acting *like* a father, just not with Kelsey?"

"It seems that way." I wince, hoping that softens the blow of my words. "Maybe you should get the whole story first."

"Oh, I will. Don't worry about that." She places her hand on top of mine and squeezes. "Just promise me you won't let this taint your view of all men, okay? Especially Daniel."

I jerk my head back. "Why would I do that?"

She cocks her brow. "Because of your history. Ever since you met Daniel, you've been hesitant to trust him, even though you didn't know him. I really want you to give him a chance, Anna. He seems like a genuinely good guy." She slips her hand from beneath mine, then leans back in her chair. "Kelsey will be prancing through the room again any minute, so I think we should table this discussion until after bedtime. Plus, I don't want to keep her waiting too long. She really wants to decorate the tree. Oh, and I have pizza coming in about ten minutes."

I perk up at the word *pizza*. "You've thought of everything."

At that, she smiles. "It's Friday night—who wants to cook? Definitely not me." She stands, then scoots her chair beneath the table. I do the same. "So, speaking of Daniel ..."

"Were we speaking of him?"

Tamara snickers. "When aren't we? Anyway, tomorrow's a big day for you two, right? You'll be hitting the town, doing good deeds ... and then what? Are you going to lunch afterward?"

I shake my head. "He didn't mention anything like that. I think it's just the volunteer work, and then we call it a day. Besides, he won't be alone. He'll have his daughter with him."

Her face falls. "Oh, I didn't think of that. Not that having her along is a bad thing, but you can't really get too deep and personal if she's listening in." She presses her lips together. "Hmm ... why don't you text me when you're almost done collecting donations? I think I have an idea."

"Oh no," I say, waving my hands between us. "You're not getting involved. I can handle this on my own."

A mischievous twinkle flashes in her eyes. "Don't you trust me?"

"I did until about two seconds ago. Now I'm not so sure."

# CHAPTER 21

# Daniel

Struggling to maneuver myself beneath the prickly Christmas tree, I finish securing the spindly trunk in the stand. Then I backwards-crawl out and stand up. Rubbing my sap-sticky palms together, I check to make sure the tree is standing straight before I go any further with my decorating endeavors.

"That looks good to me," Kurt says, his head angled to one side. "I'm glad you went with the balsam fir. That's the kind Leah and I always had growing up."

"That's why I picked it. She used to talk about the big tree hunt through the woods, and how long it would take everyone to agree on the perfect tree."

Kurt laughs. "That's because none of the trees in the woods are perfect. They look good in their natural element, but once you bring them home ..." He shakes his head. "Hey, you should do that with Madison some year. Venture out into the woods. Cut down your own tree."

I shrug. "Maybe. But I think I prefer the convenience of the tree lot."

He quirks his brow. "Have I ever told you you're too much of a city boy?"

On the other side of the room, Madison digs through the box of ornaments, and the sound raises the hair on the back of my neck. "Honey, be careful with those. Some of them are very old and breakable."

The rummaging stops. "Sorry."

"You aren't going to hang the ornaments right now, are you?" Kurt asks, rubbing a small balsam branch between two fingers. "You need to let your tree acclimate to the temperature inside and let the branches drop. Otherwise you'll end up with broken ornaments all over your floor."

I clench my jaw. Since when is Kurt the expert on Christmas tree decorating? "Madison has her heart set on decorating it tonight. I was supposed to get it last Friday, since that's our tradition, but I was ... distracted. Now that we've missed a whole week without a Christmas tree, I think I might have to take my chances and decorate it tonight."

Kurt shakes his head. "I know that keeping up with your traditions for Madison's sake is important to you, but you gotta cut yourself some slack or you'll go crazy."

"I know."

Kurt steps away from the tree, eyes it from top to bottom, then releases a long, slow breath. "Well, at least wait a little while. Have Madison pick out a Christmas movie or something."

I check the time. It is only six, so starting an hour and a half from now won't hurt anything. "Madison," I say, snagging my daughter's attention, "why don't you go pick out a movie and I'll make some popcorn? After that we can decorate the tree."

She claps her hands. "I know the best movie."

Beside me, Kurt groans. "Please don't let it be the one with the dogs who deliver presents on Christmas Eve."

I grimace. "It's either that or the one with the Christmas pageant and the depressing music. Either way, we're probably going to need a pot of coffee to go with that popcorn, or we won't make it through the night." I start toward the kitchen.

"Good idea," Kurt says as he trails behind. In the kitchen, he pulls the box of microwave popcorn from the pantry while I fill the coffee pot with water. The cellophane outer wrapper crinkles as he tears it to remove the popcorn bag. He places the unfolded bag into the microwave, then shuts the door and pushes a single button. "Hey, now that Madison's out of earshot, I meant to ask you how things are going with the art lady."

"You mean Anna?" I say over the hum of the microwave. My heart rate kicks up a notch with the mention of her name.

"Yeah, Anna. Did you ever ask her out?"

After pouring the water from the coffee pot into the reservoir, I place a filter into the basket and fill it with grounds. "I didn't ... not yet. She actually just found out about Leah. She brought up the subject, and then after that it just didn't feel like the right time."

Kurt nods while staring through the glass of the microwave door. "I get that."

"But she's coming with me when I pick up donations tomorrow morning," I say, pushing the brew button on my coffeemaker. "So that's something."

"Will Madison be with you?"

"Of course. I think it'll be a good experience for her."

"True." Kurt opens the overhead cupboard and retrieves a mug, then shuts the door. "But you need to spend time alone with Anna if you really want to get to know her." He steps forward, waving the mug in the air. "I think I can help you with that."

I step back. "By doing what?"

He grins. "Providing you with an opportunity."

"I'm a little scared to ask you what you have in mind."

He waggles his index finger in front of my face. "I wouldn't tell you even if you *did* ask. You'll just have to wait and see what I have in store for you."

"Ugh." I run both hands down my face. "Are you sure?"

"Trust me. I've got your back." He slaps my shoulder blade.

Hmm ... trust Kurt? It's not that I don't trust his intentions.

He's got a heart of gold, and I'm sure he means well, but things have a tendency to go a little sideways whenever he's involved.

Whatever his plan is, I'm sure I'll come out looking like a first-class idiot.

I probably should've kept Anna a secret for a little while longer.

# CHAPTER 22

# Daniel

During the ride over to Big Dealz on Saturday morning, I take a few minutes to prep Madison for what we'll be doing today. And also who she's going to meet. "Hey, honey, thanks for coming to help me this morning. I hope we have a lot of presents to haul, because that means that people have been very generous buying gifts for kids who need them."

She turns to me, her eyes big as saucers. "I can't wait to see!"

"Me either. But before we get there, I wanted to let you know I'm going to be meeting a friend here today, and she's going to help us deliver the gifts to St. Margaret's, where we're storing them. Her name is Anna. Would it be okay if she rides in our truck with us?"

"Yes. Is she bringing kids with her?"

I chuckle. "No, not today. But sometimes she might. She has a niece who's about your age. Maybe next time we pick up donations, she'll come along."

"Tell her she should!"

"Okay, I'll let her know you would like that."

After we pull into the parking lot, I back my pickup up to the front entrance and pull over onto the sidewalk. I leave my flashers on so no one thinks I've simply created my own front-row parking spot.

Anna is waiting for us by the entrance. She smiles as Madison and I walk up. "Well, here we are at Big Dealz again," she says. "What a difference a week makes."

"No kidding." I chuckle, trying to hide my nerves. "One week you're in the parking lot, flat on your bottom in a pile of slush with no gloves on, and the next you're here on a volunteer mission with the very man who pulled you up from that slush pile. Life is funny sometimes."

She slants her gaze toward me. "You *could* call it that."

I can't help but smile. I feel like I'm fifteen again and I'm face-to-face with the prettiest girl in school. I have the strongest urge to reach for her hand, but my daughter is standing right beside us, which is *definitely* not what it was like when I was fifteen. I'm in some weird, in-between reality.

When I notice that Anna's cheeks are red—not from embarrassment, but from the cold—I move ahead with introductions. I bend down slightly and place my hands on Madison's shoulders. "Madison, this is my new friend Anna. Anna, this is my daughter Madison."

Anna extends her hand to my daughter. "It's very nice to meet you, Madison."

"Nice to meet you too," Madison says shyly as she accepts Anna's hand, but only for a brief moment.

We make our way inside before we suffer frostbite, and immediately the decorated tree and the big box for donations comes into view. I approach the box and peer inside. There are *some* gift donations, each bagged up with a paper gingerbread ornament taped to the outside, but there are far more ornaments still left on the tree. "This isn't the huge haul I was expecting to make today."

Anna scrunches her face and motions toward the tree. "Yeah, there are still so many kids left to be chosen." Her expression brightens. "But the trees have only been up a little over a week, and there are several other drop-off locations. Maybe the other donation boxes are fuller."

"I hope so." I pull several plastic bags from the box and hand a few to Madison to carry. Anna takes what's left, and we make our way toward the exit. I nod to the employee manning the self-checkouts, nonverbally communicating to him that we're not thieves. He'll just have to trust us, I guess, since we don't have name tags or anything to indicate that we're official volunteers for the gift program.

After we load the bags into the back of my truck, I pull the soft cover over the bed and secure it before we leave Big Dealz and drive to some of the other locations. We stop at the fleet supply store, the grocery store, and then the mall, where the tree and donation box are located right in the main entrance. The amount of donations is pretty much the same at each drop-off location, which isn't very encouraging. But, like Anna said, the trees have been up for just over a week. As Christmas draws closer, people should be feeling more generous. Hopefully by next Saturday, there will be so many gifts that the boxes won't be able to hold them all.

We drive the stash we've collected to St. Margaret's, where Alvin said an old Sunday school classroom on the lower level would be available for storage. I pull up to the main entrance and, leaving Anna and Madison in the truck, I run inside to ask one of the volunteers at the homeless shelter to go downstairs and unlock the door to the lower level. Then I pull my truck around to the back of the building and park along the curb so we can unload. Madison unbuckles herself, then pops out of the crew cab just as Anna pushes open the passenger-side door. Together we haul what we've collected into the church's basement and leave it in the classroom the volunteer said would be best.

St. Margaret's hasn't functioned as a church in over a decade. For the last few years, its main floor has housed the only homeless shelter in Lake Valley. It's manned entirely by volunteers twenty-four hours a day, and there is very little reason why anyone would use this lower-level entry door—although it would be an easy way for someone to sneak in without others knowing. So when we're ready to leave and I realize the door doesn't lock without a key, I turn to Anna. "I'm going to pop upstairs and let someone know that we're finished with our delivery and they need to relock the basement door."

"That's a good idea," she says. "I can wait in the truck with Madison."

"Great. Thanks." No sooner do I hand Anna my keys than Kurt appears, rounding the corner from the direction of the upper parking lot. My jaw drops at the unexpected sight of him.

His eyes widen in what looks like surprise, but I know better. He knew he'd find me here. "Oh, hey, Daniel. What a totally random coincidence to run into you."

Anna eyes Kurt with scrutiny before turning a questioning gaze on me.

I toss my hands out to my sides, nonverbally answering her look with one of my own that says *I have no idea*.

"Kurt," I say once he's stopped in front of me. "What are you doing here?"

He clears his throat. "I was just driving around and thought I might go out for some ice cream."

I fold my arms across my chest. The only ice cream shop in town is nowhere near here. "Did you get lost?"

He laughs while nodding his head. "Yeah, I must've gotten turned around. But it's a good thing, right? I haven't had a chance to meet your new friend, and now here we all are." His gaze sweeps over to Anna, and he gives her a charming smile while holding out his hand. "I'm Kurt, Daniel's brother-in-law. You must be Anna."

I run my fingers through my hair as I watch them shake hands, all the while silently praying that Kurt doesn't blow this for me. What if Anna thinks *I* set this up? If she knew Kurt, this wouldn't surprise her at all, but she doesn't know him. She barely knows *me*.

Kurt takes a step back and motions to Madison, then to me. "Hey, I just had the greatest idea. I know how much Madison loves the homemade waffle cones at the ice cream shop. Do you mind if she comes with me?" He looks down at my daughter and winks. "I'll get you a three-scoop cone."

"Two scoops," I say without missing a beat. "I mean, if you want to go, Madison. Otherwise you can ride home with me. Like we planned."

She jumps up and down, her fisted hands held close to her chest. "I want ice cream!"

Of course she does, just like Kurt knew she would. I feel like I no longer have any say in my own life.

Kurt wags his index finger between Anna and me. "Well, now that you two will be all alone, you should ... I don't know, go somewhere. Together." He bobs his head in a very self-satisfied way, clearly proud of his brilliant plan.

I open my mouth to respond, but don't get a word out because a silver minivan slows to a stop beside the curb, right behind my truck. The front passenger-side window rolls down, and the driver, a woman I know I've seen before, leans across the center console. In the back seat I can see a little girl, and I recognize her as the same girl that Anna brought with her to City Hall. It's her niece. Ah, yes. So the driver is Anna's sister, the one I met at the mall.

This situation is starting to get painful.

"Hey, guys," Anna's sister says, leaning forward to see through the open window.

Beside me, Anna shakes her head while walking toward her sister's vehicle. "Tamara? What are *you* doing here?"

Tamara. That's right.

"Kelsey was getting a little bored this morning, so I told her I'd take her to the movie theater to watch that new animated film, the one about the penguin family who hitches a ride on a cruise ship from the Galapagos Islands all the way to the North Pole to get a message to Santa Claus. It plays at noon. You wouldn't happen to know of any little girls who might want to come to the movies with us, would you?"

I place my hand over my mouth and shake my head. This woman is even more obvious than Kurt. And the plot of that movie sounds so implausible, I can't even wrap my head around it.

"Um ..." Anna looks down at Madison, then back at her sister. "This is Daniel's daughter, Madison. I *think* she's on her way to get ice cream, so I'm not sure—"

"Hey," Kurt says, stepping forward and bending down to peer through the open window. "I'm Kurt. Nice to meet you. How about you guys join us? Everyone loves ice cream, right? Or we could go to the movies and then out for ice cream."

"That's a great idea," Tamara says. "Let's do both. We'll meet you at the theater in ten minutes."

I slant my gaze toward Anna and she looks at me with wide eyes. We have lost control here.

I hold up both hands. "Look, you guys do not have to do this. I know we're all busy, and you probably have better things to do than watch movies about penguins."

"No way," Kurt says as he straightens to his full height. He presses a hand to Madison's shoulder and guides her to the sidewalk. "We're going, regardless of what you do. So you might as well make the most of it. And take your time. Don't hurry back." He takes Madison's hand and leads her up the hill toward the parking lot.

Inside the car, Tamara smiles and waves. "Have fun, you two." Before Anna or I can respond, the passenger-side window rolls up and she pulls away.

I turn to Anna and raise my eyebrows. "What just happened?"

She shrugs. "I think we've been set up, and now Kurt and my sister are going on a playdate together."

I can't help shaking my head. "That was so obvious. They didn't even try to play it cool."

"I'd go so far as to call it cringe-worthy."

"Agreed."

I stare at Anna while shifting my weight from one leg to the other. "So, now that it's just you and me, should we ... I don't know, grab some coffee or something?"

It doesn't take long for her smile to overtake her entire face. "It sounds like we have all afternoon. Let's go crazy and have coffee *and* lunch." Then, without another word, she practically skips to my truck and hops inside.

Even though the last ten minutes have been some of the most awkward of my life, I have to admit I owe Kurt big time for this.

# CHAPTER 23

# *Anna*

After Daniel informs the volunteers at St. Margaret's that we're leaving, he drives us to Up North Panini, a small café known for both their sandwiches and their lattes. It's a newer business, but it's quickly becoming one of my favorite local spots. We order at the counter, then take a number and find a seat by the window.

Daniel fidgets with his hands and shifts in his seat for a minute before finally meeting my gaze. "So, I just want you to know this isn't how I planned our first date to go."

I tilt my head to one side. "Oh, is this a date? I didn't realize."

A flush of red spreads across his cheeks. "Uh … no." He reaches a hand up to rub the back of his neck. "I didn't mean that *this* was a date. Only that if it were, I would've gone about it in a different way."

I press my lips together to keep my smile from overtaking my face, only because he's so adorable when he's nervous—and he is *so* clearly nervous. "Daniel, there's no pressure. If it's too soon for this to be a date, then it's not one. I'm just glad to be here with you, and it doesn't matter what we call this or how we ended up here in the first place."

He exhales a whoosh of air while shaking his head. "Thanks

for understanding. Look, Anna, I've wanted to ask you out since the day we met, but ..." He looks down at his hands, folded on the tabletop. "I haven't spent time with *any* woman other than my assistant since Leah passed."

I so badly want to reach for his hands and cover them with my own, but after what he just said, I think it would be too much too soon. "Let's just take things one day at a time, okay?"

The server comes to deliver our sandwiches and coffees to the table, and I hardly notice, because all I can focus on is the fact that Daniel is so ... *incredible,* and that he's the exact opposite of how I'd first pegged him. Maybe I have managed to find a decent guy who isn't going to lie to me. Someone who is who he says he is and doesn't have a secret, alternate personality when I'm not around.

Daniel centers his plate in front of him and clears his throat. "So, I wanted to explain what happened on Black Friday."

I shake my head. "You don't have to explain. I completely understand."

"I know, but if we're going to continue our ... *friendship,* which technically started that day, I feel like I need to at least clear a few things up."

"Okay," I say, holding my hands up. "For the sake of our friendship, go ahead."

He shifts in his seat and looks down for a moment before returning his gaze to meet mine. "Christmas shopping was always Leah's job. She loved doing it and she was great at it. Last Christmas I was on my own for the first time, and I royally messed up buying gifts for Madison. I know she's young and it shouldn't matter what gifts she receives, but it mattered to me. It was one more reminder that she didn't have her mom anymore, and that I wasn't good at doing what Leah did. So when the holiday season rolled around again this year, I wanted to make at least one thing better—buying the perfect Christmas gift. I didn't want to let my little girl down a second time."

I bite my lower lip and nod. "I get that. I was feeling a similar pressure that morning to buy the gift my niece wanted most. She's had a rough few months."

"Do you mind if I ask what's been going on?" Daniel says.

I lift my shoulder in a half shrug. "My sister and Kelsey's father were never married. They had a pretty rocky relationship, and he walked out on them for good when Kelsey was just a few months old. Ever since then, he's been in and out of their lives, working for months at a time out of state with the pipeline. Even though he sends money every once in a while, my sister is pretty much on her own. A few months ago, Tamara started working nights at the hospital. It was a pay raise, but it made finding a babysitter difficult, since it involved overnight stays. That's why I moved back home."

"Ah," Daniel says. "I'm really glad you're here in Lake Valley, but I'm sorry it's not under the best circumstances."

"It's okay. I'm glad to be back too. I've missed my sister, and I'm the only other family that Kelsey has." I swallow to keep my emotions from tightening my throat. "Wayne—my sister's ex— told Kelsey he would be home for Thanksgiving this year, and she was really looking forward to seeing him. Then at the last minute, he backed out, and she was crushed. When I met you on Black Friday, I was highly motivated to get that TeddyTab for Kelsey because she's had so many disappointments lately. I didn't want her Christmas gift to be another one. Unfortunately, I was so focused on that goal, I didn't consider the fact that other people may have had really good reasons for wanting the same thing that I wanted." I look straight into his eyes. "I'm sorry, again, for seeing you as an obstacle rather than a real person."

He looks at me and smiles, his dimples showing beneath a fine layer of stubble. "You're more than forgiven."

As we stare at each other, the air between us pulsates with energy. I don't know what to say next, but Daniel's gaze is so intense, I have to break eye contact. As a distraction, I reach for my coffee and bring the cup to my lips. The sight of the creamy brown liquid only reminds me more of the morning when I first met Daniel, and how his eyes mesmerized me.

I set the cup down without taking a sip, then tap the side of my cup with my fingernail. "You know, you're not the only one here who's a little apprehensive about starting a new relationship—not that this is a relationship, because clearly we've defined this as a friendship, and that's totally okay with me. I'm fine with moving slow. The last time I allowed myself to fall for someone, I ended up getting hurt. Turns out I didn't *really* know him as well as I thought, and I vowed not to let it happen again."

He rubs his jaw. "Is there anything about me that makes you apprehensive?"

Only the fact that I've never felt such a strong connection to someone so quickly after meeting them—but no way am I telling him that. "No," I say with a shake of my head. "Every doubt I had stemmed from my own misconceptions. So far, you haven't given me a real reason not to trust you." Thanks to men like Brady and Wayne, I've had a slightly tainted view of men and relationships. But I'm not going to let them continue to ruin things for me. "I do trust you, Daniel. Just promise me you won't ever lie to me."

He leans forward and looks into my eyes. "You have my word on that. I will always be honest with you."

I arrive home several hours later, and Tamara pulls into the driveway right beside me. The large garage door goes up and we pull in, one after the other, and park side by side. "That was perfect timing," I say, stepping out of my car. The back door of the minivan slides open and Kelsey hops out. "How did your little outing go?" I ask her. "Did you like the movie?"

Kelsey beams. "It was so funny. The baby penguin is seasick the whole time."

I grimace. That doesn't sound so funny to me.

"After the movie," Kelsey continues, "I got ice cream with chocolate syrup *and* sprinkles. And Madison got strawberry."

My brow lifts. "Ah, so you made a new friend. Do you like Madison?"

Kelsey nods, then runs for the door that leads into the house.

Tamara walks around the front of her vehicle, and she follows me toward the door that Kelsey left wide open. "The more important question is, do you like Madison's daddy?" Her words drip with insinuation.

I side-eye Tamara as I climb the two steps up into the house. "I think we've already established that. Now no more embarrassing matchmaking schemes. We can take it from here."

"Oh, that's too bad," she says, closing the door. "Because we've already arranged another play date for the girls."

"We?"

"Yeah, Kurt and I. Next Saturday, you and Daniel will drive around town collecting donations, and you'll bring both girls with you."

"Oh, do you work that day?" I ask.

"Nope. But you need a reason to spend time with him beyond the weekly gift collection. That takes, what, an hour?"

I mentally review the events of this morning. "Almost two hours."

"Well, that's not enough time. So Kurt and I thought you two needed a little push. I'll make lunch while you're gone, and you, Daniel, and the girls can stop over here to eat. Then the girls can play for a few hours, and I'll make myself scarce."

"Will Kurt be here as well?" I ask.

She shakes her head. "No. And before you get any ideas, I'm not interested in him. He's just helping me with this little side gig, because we both have the same goal—to see our loved ones happy. And to be honest, I don't know what Kurt does for a living. He says he 'dabbles' in real estate, but he was pretty vague about what that meant. I'm looking for stability. He is a great guy, though, which is important since he'll be part of your family when you and Daniel get married. If nothing else, he'll make the holidays fun."

I throw my head back and laugh. "Tamara! You are getting so far ahead of yourself. Daniel and I have known each other one week and one day. We've been on one date, and he was a little too skittish to call it a date, so I think it's too soon to be thinking about marriage."

"You can't tell me *you* haven't thought about it." Her eyebrows bounce up and down.

I chop my hand through the air. "We're done here. Supper's in the crock pot. You and Kelsey can eat whenever you want. Meanwhile, I'll be hiding in my room."

# CHAPTER 24

# Daniel

The past week has been crazy busy. I've had endless calls and meetings with members of the food bank's building committee in preparation for the posting of construction bids early in the new year. With the groundbreaking expected to start around late April—or whenever the ground is thawed—there isn't a lot of extra time.

And on top of that, Madison had a cold. Not a bad one, but she did miss school for a couple days due to her fever, so I worked from home. Needless to say, I didn't get a whole lot done while taking care of a sick first grader.

Today is Saturday, so I can finally see Anna. We've been texting a lot these last few days. Just quick little messages here and there, checking in to see how the other is doing, but it's never enough. I still can't believe how things have progressed between us in a matter of days. I'm excited for what the future holds, and I haven't felt that way in a long time. Anna and I are still throwing around the whole "friendship" title like a safety net or a protective vest—something that will cushion us from the blow if things don't work out. But for some reason, the idea of diving in isn't as scary as it used to be.

I find myself humming as I make breakfast for Madison. I

never hum. Especially Christmas carols. I wipe my hands on a dish towel, then wad it up and toss it on the counter like I'm making a free throw.

Anna had mentioned that both girls would be joining us on our gift collection route this morning—a plan concocted by Tamara and Kurt, which Kurt failed to mention. But I won't hold it against him. I'm just relieved that he's being supportive. I wouldn't feel right pursuing Anna without his blessing.

At nine thirty, Madison and I pick up Anna and Kelsey at their house, and then we spend almost two hours driving from one donation location to the next. This time we find double the amount of gifts piled inside each donation box compared to the week before. When we arrive at St. Margaret's, I actually sigh in relief. My truck bed couldn't possibly hold any more without something getting smashed or broken.

I pull up to the front door and park. "I'll need the basement door unlocked again," I say. "There are so many more bags this time, and I really don't think they'd want us parading all of these presents through the shelter."

"I suppose not," Anna agrees. "I'll wait here with the girls."

"I want to go in with you," Madison says.

"So do I." That was Kelsey. Of course if Madison comes inside, she'll want to come in too.

I sigh. "Okay, we can all go inside and ask the nice volunteer to open up the downstairs door for us."

I lead our little troop through the main entry and into the lobby of St. Margaret's. As soon as we enter, we're met by a volunteer staff member, the same one I talked to a week ago. "Hi, again," I say, pulling my stocking cap off my head and stuffing it into my coat pocket. "I'm here to drop off gifts for storage in your basement again, if that's okay."

The woman smiles and nods. "Of course. Just pull around back and I'll meet you at the door."

"Thank you." I start to turn when I notice Madison's wide eyes. She's taking in her surroundings with intense interest.

"What is this building, Daddy? It doesn't look like a church on the inside."

I follow her line of sight to the set of double doors that are open to what used to be the sanctuary. Inside the spacious room, the pews have been removed and replaced with rows and rows of bunk beds. I glance down the hall and notice more rooms—bedrooms with curtain doors, which I assume are set aside for families.

I bend down to meet her at her level. "This is called a homeless shelter. It's where people stay when they don't have anywhere else to live. It keeps them safe and out of the cold."

"Why wouldn't they have anywhere to live?" she asks.

I glance up at Anna, then over to Kelsey, who is also very interested in what she's seeing. I haven't had a chance to have this kind of conversation with Madison, and I feel underprepared. I always thought she was a bit young to talk about things of such a serious nature, but I'm certain there are kids her age and younger staying here. At least for now. Madison should know that not everyone has a cozy, warm bed to crawl into at night, or three square meals provided for them every day.

I stand up and take my daughter's hand. "Honey, we have to meet the nice lady who's opening the door for us downstairs. After we unload gifts, I'll tell you all about the homeless shelter."

I drive the truck down to the lower level and back up so the bed is facing the door. The volunteer, Sharon, helps us carry the bags of gifts to the unused classroom we've been using to store them. Once all of the donations have been unloaded, I smile at Sharon. "Thanks for your help. I'm glad you have this room for us to store these gifts. Otherwise, I'm afraid they'd all end up in my basement."

She shakes her head while smiling back at me. "It's no problem at all. We have the extra space. The basement here at St. Margaret's is a little too dark and cold to use for housing, so we use the upstairs where there's plenty of room and a whole lot more sunlight."

"Is the entire basement just empty space, then?" Anna asks.

Sharon wildly waves a hand through the air. "No, we do use most of this lower level for storage. We keep the supply room down here. When we receive donations of everyday supplies like toilet paper, soap, and shampoo, we store them just down the hall." She extends her left hand. "Would you like to see?"

I look down at Kelsey and Madison, who seem more than eager to follow this stranger down a dark hallway. "Uh ... sure," I say, placing a hand on Madison's shoulder. This could be quite a learning experience for her, and it may help answer some of her questions about the homeless—or lead to dozens more.

Sharon pulls the coiled key chain from her wrist and unlocks another door. She flips on the light, revealing walls of shelves and boxes piled high. On one end of the room is a clothes rack with coats in all sizes and colors hanging from it. On another rack hangs an assortment of backpacks.

"When people come to us in the winter, they don't always have the proper outdoor clothing," Sharon says. "We try to have coats, hats, mittens, and boots in a variety of sizes on hand. When people leave, we like to send them off as well prepared as possible." She shakes her head. "We recently met a six-year-old boy who showed up wearing an adult extra-large fleece jacket. The poor boy was practically lost in it. And he had no boots. Just sneakers with holes in the bottoms, and they were wet from walking through the snow to get here."

I imagine my daughter wearing a coat that's one size bigger than what I wear. She would trip over it. And not to have boots during a Minnesota winter? The thought sends chills up my spine.

"Are the backpacks for school?" I ask.

"Actually," Sharon says, "a lot of the kids come carrying every-thing they own in a backpack—all their worldly possessions—which means they can't have a lot, or it would be too heavy to carry. If their backpacks are in rough shape, we offer them new ones."

"Why do they carry all their things in a backpack?" Madison asks, her eyes wide.

"Well," Sharon says in a sweet voice, "it depends on what their previous living situation was, but so many of them don't have anywhere else to store their things."

Anna walks slowly along the row of coats, gently touching each one as she passes. "How long can people stay here at the shelter?"

"Generally, people are allowed to stay here for up to thirty days. During that time we try to better prepare them for independent living. In our resource center, they can find information on employment and housing opportunities."

Anna reaches the end of the row of hanging coats, then turns back to face the rest of us. "Where do they come from mostly? I've never seen people living on the streets here in Lake Valley."

Sharon shrugs. "We take in people who've been sleeping in their cars, staying at motels, and people who have been evicted from their apartments. Some have just left treatment facilities and others have been released from jail and have nowhere to go once they're free. But the majority of folks have been staying with friends or family."

Kelsey walks over to a box that's full of children's books. She pulls one out and shows it to Madison.

"Those are donations for our children's library. We still haven't gotten around to unloading them."

"It sounds like you have a lot of children here," I say.

Sharon nods. "Unfortunately, yes. This may be surprising, but children make up a large portion of the homeless population."

Anna places a hand to her chest. "Oh my."

Sharon gives us sad smile. "Because of that, we are always accepting donations of kids' clothing here at the shelter, so if you know of anyone with lots of kids, we'll take their hand-me-downs. Of all the clothes we offer, it's usually the underwear that the kids are most excited about. I found that surprising when I first started helping here."

Wow. Underwear? Who would've thought? I never expected a quick trip to drop off donations would turn into such an eye-opening experience. I'm glad my daughter is here, seeing what I'm seeing. I glance over at her, standing quietly beside her new friend Kelsey, and my thoughts instantly turn to the TeddyTab. My heart lurches. Some kids get excited to own a clean pair of underwear, while a little over a week ago, I was nearly wrestling with Anna over an expensive, electronic teddy bear so Madison could ... what, play video games on it? While little children their age walk through the snow with holes in their shoes, carrying everything they own in a small backpack, I'm worried that a two-hundred-dollar toy isn't enough to make my daughter happy? Of course it's not enough, because material things only bring temporary happiness, and happiness isn't true joy.

*Joy to the world, the Lord has come.*

The familiar refrain plays through my mind, reminding me that Christmas isn't about happiness. It's about joy—joy that comes not from whatever presents are under the tree, but from the one who entered our world as a tiny baby in order to save us from our sins and offer us eternal life.

I run a hand through my hair and turn in time to catch Anna staring at me while wiping a tear from her eye. Seeing the look on her face, I suspect she just might be thinking the same thing that I am.

After our brief tour of the supply room, Anna and I thank Sharon. She locks up behind us as we usher the girls out into the cold. None of us speaks a word, because no words are needed. The experience we'd just shared spoke volumes.

Halfway to Anna's house, I break the silence. "So, what'd you think?"

Anna turns to me and places her hand on my arm, giving it a gentle squeeze and making my heart beat triple-time. "I think Tamara and I need to have a talk."

# CHAPTER 25

# Anna

Tamara has made a crockpot full of tomato soup using the Roma tomatoes she grew in her garden over the summer, then canned. She's serving it alongside grilled cheese sandwiches, which she's piled high on a plate in the center of the dining table.

"Okay, guys," she says. "Eat up. I can keep making more sandwiches as long as you're still hungry."

"Thank you so much for having us over," Daniel says. "I feel spoiled. Most days it's just me and Madison at our house, and lunch usually consists of macaroni and cheese or peanut butter and jelly sandwiches."

Tamara's head tilts. "This is just grilled cheese. It's hardly gourmet."

"Don't sell yourself short," Daniel says. "This homemade soup is amazing."

When Kelsey and Madison are finished eating, Kelsey asks to be excused from the table so she can show Madison her collection of plastic horses. "Madison loves horses too," she says. "We want to play with them in my room."

"Go ahead," Tamara says, finally unplugging the griddle after making about a dozen sandwiches. "Just carry your dishes to the sink first."

Once the girls have left the room, Tamara slumps into the seat next to me across from Daniel. She wipes the back of her hand across her brow. "So, how was your day? Were there many donations this time?"

I nod. "About double what we collected last week."

Tamara's eyes light up. "That's great. I'm sure people just needed to get Black Friday out of their minds and start focusing more on the bigger picture of Christmas, rather than just getting a good deal. As Christmas draws closer, people tend to start thinking more about others."

I sit up straighter, then clear my throat. "Um, it's funny you should mention that, because I want to talk to you about something."

Tamara's brow deepens to form a *V* between her eyes. "Okay ... what's up?"

I fold my hands in front of me. "Well, we all know that what Kelsey really wants, more than anything else, is to see her dad."

Tamara rolls her eyes. "Yeah, and now who knows when that will happen."

"Right. And even a TeddyTab won't alleviate the pain of that disappointment. Not really."

"What are you saying, Anna?" Tamara looks at me, then Daniel, and then back at me.

I shift in my seat. "I'm saying ... are you sure Kelsey really needs a TeddyTab? And if so, why? It won't bring back her dad, and it won't fill the space in her heart that he left empty."

Tamara leans back and crosses her arms. "I never said it would."

I can tell she's putting up her defenses, and it breaks my heart to know that I'm the one making her feel the need to. I lean forward. "Hear me out, Tam. Today we were at St. Margaret's and we spent some time talking to one of the volunteers. You should have heard her stories about how the families—the kids—show up without proper clothing. Some of them have to live in their cars while they wait for an opening at the shelter. They have nothing. Literally nothing. Our community is pulling together to donate gifts to children in need, and they're asked to spend ten to twenty dollars on each gift. Ten to twenty dollars, Tamara. And we have a two-hundred-dollar bear for one child sitting in the closet down the hall. With the money from that one bear, we could buy gifts for up to twenty kids who otherwise might not get anything else on Christmas morning."

Tamara looks me square in the eyes. "So what do you want? Do you want to return the bear?"

"Technically Daniel would have to return it, but ... yeah. Maybe. But not until you talk to Kelsey. Ask her if she really wants a TeddyTab. It's very possible that some of the other kids in her class were drawing TeddyTabs in their journals, and she just went along with it. You know how kids copy each other. I honestly haven't heard Kelsey mention a word about TeddyTabs since that day at the mall when she sat on Santa's lap."

Tamara sighs loudly. "I haven't either."

"Even if Daniel returns the one he bought, we would still have the rain check to buy one after Christmas if you change your mind. Of course Kelsey is your daughter, so it's your call. You're the one who decides."

Tamara rubs her forehead. "I know the bear would make Kelsey happy, but only for a little while. That's the way it works with kids and toys, right? The newness wears off, and they move on to the next thing."

"Typically, yes."

Tamara drops her palms to the tabletop, fingertips tapping for a few seconds. "Listen, everything you're saying makes sense to me. I just need to think about this for a little while."

"I completely understand," I say.

"And if I do decide we should return the bear, what will we get Kelsey? I don't want her to have nothing to open on

Christmas morning, but I also don't want to buy a bunch of meaningless gifts just so she has something under the tree."

Daniel hesitantly raises his hand. "I think I can help with that. I have an idea."

True to her word, Tamara made herself scarce after lunch, giving Daniel and me a chance to talk uninterrupted for a couple of hours while the girls played horses and mermaids and who knows what else.

I learned more about Daniel's family, his mom and dad, who live in southern Minnesota, and about Leah and her family, who, although they're natives of Lake Valley, I never knew personally. Daniel seems comfortable talking about his wife around me, and for that I'm grateful. She was a huge part of his life and always will be. If we're ever going to be more than friends, I want to know everything about him. So far, the more I know, the more I want to know. There is nothing I've learned about Daniel Hawkins that I don't like.

In the evening, after Daniel and Madison leave for home, Tamara finds me in the kitchen prepping for supper. She sidles up beside me and takes over the job of cubing potatoes, allowing me to move on to something else.

"You and Daniel seemed cozy on the couch," she teases.

I scoff. "Were you spying on us?"

"No, but I may have passed by the living room once or twice on my way to check in on the girls." She pauses her chopping and turns to me. "I'm glad we had him over. If you're going to date him, I want to get to know him better. So far, I'm very impressed."

I reach for the vegetable peeler on the counter and slide it across the surface of a carrot. "I am too. I like him more each time I see him."

We work silently side by side for a few minutes until Tamara clears her throat. "So, I talked to Kelsey about the TeddyTab." She keeps her eyes focused on her cutting board.

"Oh?" Doing my best to appear unaffected, I slice away at my carrot, even though its outermost layer has been thoroughly removed. I'm not going to pressure my sister to decide one way or another when it comes to the TeddyTab, although the anticipation of what she's going to say sends my heart rate skyrocketing.

Tamara makes two more chops with her knife before setting it down. "She said that's what all the kids in her class are getting—or at least it's what they're all asking for."

"Did she say *she* wanted one?"

Tamara shakes her head. "She said it didn't really matter." She chuckles. "And here I was so worried that not getting one would crush her. Now it seems like it was never a big deal to begin with."

"Good thing you asked her then."

"Definitely. You can go ahead and tell Daniel to return the bear."

I turn to face her. "Are you sure?"

She nods. "When you step back and look at this from a different perspective, it does seem a bit extreme. I mean, she's five. Kids spend enough time on electronic devices when they get older, and the fact that this one comes disguised as a teddy bear doesn't make it any less of a tech gadget. It's just softer on one side. A regular teddy bear might be a better option."

I take a hesitant sidestep toward Tamara and place a hand on her shoulder. "I know you just want to get Kelsey something she'll really love for Christmas. Who knows—maybe Wayne will shock us all by showing up on Christmas morning with a TeddyTab for her."

Tamara scoffs. "I wouldn't hold my breath. And I don't know that I want him to give her one, either. After hearing what you said about the children at the homeless shelter, and the families who are participating in the gift program so their kids can get *something* for Christmas, it all seems excessive. Now I almost feel sick to my stomach at the thought of giving Kelsey something so expensive at her age."

"That's why I think Daniel's idea is so great. It's not something you can buy at a store. He's making it. Apparently he made one for Madison, and she plays with it every day."

"And still you've failed to tell me what it is. Are you two going to keep me in the dark until Christmas? The gift isn't for me, you know."

"True, but don't you want to be surprised when Kelsey opens it?"

Tamara shakes her head. "Not really. Christmas isn't that far away, and we just decided to return Kelsey's only gift. I'd like to know that I can relax and not worry about trying to find something to replace it."

I suddenly notice how tense she is. "Of course. I'm sorry we didn't tell you sooner. Daniel wants to build a horse stable for Kelsey to put her play horses in. What do you think of that idea?"

Tamara leans back against the counter. "Oh wow. That *is* a great gift. Maybe I can get her another little horse to go with it."

I clasp my hands together. "I'll tell Daniel to get started on it. He'll be so happy. And Kelsey's going to love it."

# CHAPTER 26

# *Anna*

The high-pitched cackling of ladies having way too much fun for a Monday morning spills out of the 2D studio. Meanwhile, I'm staring at my computer screen with my fingers pressed against my ears, trying to block out the noise so I can concentrate.

Carla crosses the room and stops across the desk from me. She tilts her head in an appraising look. "There are only twelve days until Christmas. Don't tell me you're still trying to find another one of those TeddyTabs."

"No, I'm not. I've actually decided to return the one I have to the store. Well, Daniel will have to return it, because he bought it. We've decided to go an entirely different direction with our Christmas shopping this year."

Carla's brows rise. "We? You and Daniel are buying joint gifts? After two dates?"

My cheeks burn with embarrassment. "No, we've both decided *separately* to go in a different direction, meaning neither of us is giving a TeddyTab to anyone this year."

"That's an interesting turn of events. So if you're not searching for the year's hottest toy, what *are* you looking for? I haven't seen you so focused on your computer screen since Black Friday."

I straighten my spine and smile. "Since the auction was such a success this year, and we were able to donate to a worthy cause like the food bank, I'm thinking we could make the auction a yearly event. I'm looking for ideas for next November. If we keep the same date, which falls just after National Homelessness and Hunger Awareness Week, I think we should keep the theme the same as well. Maybe next year the profits could go toward affordable housing."

"That sounds like quite an undertaking. Did you find some viable options?"

"I did. You would not believe the small, portable house kits that you can purchase for less than $1,500."

Carla walks around to my side of the desk. "How many house kits were you thinking?"

"That would depend on how much money we raise." I point to a picture on the screen. "These housing units are very basic, but they can hold a family of six, and they provide a dry place for them to store their things while they're out looking for jobs or going to school."

"Wow, the auction sure has inspired you," Carla says.

I shake my head. "It wasn't just the auction. On Saturday, Daniel and I were at St. Margaret's, and we spent some time talking to a volunteer. Before I started collecting donations for the children's gift program, I had never set foot in the homeless shelter before."

"I'm sure most people haven't."

"Well maybe they should. It was eye-opening for me. Did you know that so many homeless children don't even have a teddy bear because everything they own has to be carried around on their backs?"

"Uh ... no, I did not. And to think, just a couple of weeks ago you were fighting with a man over who got to keep a two-hundred-dollar teddy bear. Seems kind of petty now, doesn't it?"

My breath hitches.

Carla winces. "I'm sorry. That was harsh."

"No, don't apologize. You're exactly right. I had the same thoughts, and so did Daniel. It was like everything got put into perspective for us, and I'm glad it did." I rise from my stool and begin pacing. "Kelsey has so much. Yes, her dad needs a giant mallet to the side of the head, and I don't know what's going to happen with that, but she still has a family. Tamara and I love her to death. And she has a home. It's no mansion, but at least it's warm and dry, and Kelsey has a bed, and food, and underwear."

Carla quirks a brow.

"Yes, underwear. Something we all take for granted."

"Not all of us."

I roll my eyes. "The point is, an expensive toy won't fill the void her dad has left, but maybe showing love to others will help her understand God's love for her." I tap my finger on the edge of my desk. "I think we should all sign up to pack boxes at the food bank next Friday, the seventeenth. They're running low on volunteers because of the holidays, and they're struggling to get all of the holiday meal boxes packed before Christmas. I don't want a single family in Lake Valley to go without a decent Christmas dinner."

"I would love to help," Carla says. "What time is this food-boxing?"

"We can sign up for any block of two or three hours at a time, but they're only open until five. We could close the gallery for a couple of hours or have Laura or one of the other teachers man the desk."

"If we put a sign on the door saying why we're closed, I don't think anyone will complain," Carla says. "We're not especially busy this time of year."

I wave my hand through the air. "Maybe. We'll figure it out. I'm sure Daniel can round up a few folks as well. With you, me, and Tamara—plus the girls—I think we'll have quite a packing crew. I can't wait to tell Alvin Reed."

Carla props her hands on her hips and shakes her head. "I haven't seen you this excited about anything in a long time."

"To be honest, there hasn't been a whole lot to be excited about. My sister's raising a child on her own. Kelsey's dad left and barely communicates with her. I was so focused on all the things that had been going wrong, I forgot to look for the blessings in my life—and there are so many! I really want to help Kelsey and Tamara see those blessings, too."

*Thank you, Lord, for opening my eyes.*

# CHAPTER 27

# Daniel

The volunteer hours have really added up this week, but that also means I'm spending more and more time with Anna, so I can't complain. In total, there are eight of us involved in the children's gift program, and we're all doing different tasks in order to get these gifts to the right kids and make sure that no one is left out.

Tomorrow is Saturday, and it's our final day to collect gifts around town. Any kids whose ornaments are still hanging on trees by that point will still need gifts, and it will be our job to buy them so they're ready in time for the distribution day on Monday the twentieth.

But before I can even think about tomorrow's gift collection and shopping spree, I need to focus on today, because it's food-boxing day at the food bank. I'm closing up the office for the afternoon, and Lois and I are both heading over to the food bank. On my way, I have to pick up Madison early from school. She's excited about this little field trip, and I am too—I think it'll be a good experience for her.

Kurt is meeting us there, and so are Anna, Tamara, and Kelsey. With Alvin Reed and several volunteers from the county's Child and Family Services Department, we have a total crew of twelve people. I'm hoping to get quite a few holiday food boxes filled up during our three-hour shift.

I'm running a few minutes behind, so I hurry to open the door for Madison, and then check in at the front desk. When the receptionist looks up, her eyes brighten. "Ah, Daniel. Are you here for another walk-through?"

I shake my head and place a hand on Madison's shoulder. "Actually, I'm here as a volunteer today. My daughter and I are packing food boxes."

"That's great. We really need the help." She taps her pen against the clipboard on her desk. "I assume you're with the group that's about to start orientation right now. Just write your names on the sign-in sheet and then you can head on into the warehouse."

"Thanks. Have a good day." As I sign my name, I notice Anna's name just a few lines above mine. My chest tightens as nervous energy courses through my veins. I've seen her almost every day this week, but I'm still excited to see her again today.

I push open the heavy door to the warehouse and let Madison step through before I follow behind. The temperature is at least ten degrees cooler in this big open space than in the lobby, which I should've remembered, having been here numerous times before. I'm always warm, especially when I'm working, but Madison's small body doesn't run as hot as mine. I wish I'd brought a jacket for her, or maybe even a stocking cap.

The dial on my daddy guilt meter rises a little higher.

I take Madison's hand as we walk past three long rows of shelving, and there, in the corner, I see the group of volunteers gathered beside a forklift. Bill, the food bank's warehouse manager, is standing in the middle of everyone explaining something, but I can't hear a word over all the background noise.

When Anna looks up and sees me, she smiles. I squeeze into the circle beside her, while Madison gallops up to Kelsey and grabs her around the waist. The two girls jump up and down—

probably more excited to be let out of school early than to be packing boxes.

I must be the last person to arrive, because once I've found my place, Bill begins explaining what we'll be doing today.

"In each box, you'll place the basic ingredients for a full holiday meal. The boxes come flat and unfolded, so we'll need someone at the beginning of the line to assemble them. Once that person has secured the bottom of the box with packing tape, they'll set it on the conveyor and roll it down the line to the next person, who will place their item inside before passing the box to the next, and so on. Along the line, you'll fill the box with one cardboard carton of milk, two cans of green beans, a jar of applesauce, a large can of sweet potatoes, one can of cranberry sauce, a jug of apple juice, and a box of stuffing mix. When we distribute the boxes to the families, they'll also receive a smoked ham, a five-pound bag of potatoes, and an apple pie."

Heads nod all around and a murmur of agreement fills the air.

Bill gestures toward Alvin Reed, who's standing at the very end of the line. "Once a box is full, our fearless leader, Alvin, will fold the top flaps and tape it shut. He'll place the full boxes on the pallet here." He points to the pallet at the end of the conveyor. "Each pallet holds forty-five boxes—five rows of nine boxes each. I'd like to get four pallets full, if not five."

I gulp. That's a lot of boxes. I edge closer to Anna. "Do you think we'll be able to get that many boxes packed?"

She looks up at me and shrugs. "I'm willing to try—as long as you don't distract me from my duties."

"I wouldn't dare." I gently nudge her arm with my elbow.

Kurt volunteers to assemble boxes on the far end of the conveyor, and I follow him down the narrow aisle between the conveyor and the food pallets until I locate the boxed milk. On the shelf above is a piece of paper with a number *one*, indicating that one carton of milk goes into each food box. I turn to Anna, who's now standing beside me. "I guess I'm the milkman," I say with a wink. "What are you?"

She looks behind her to the pallet stacked with rows and rows of aluminum cans, then turns back to me. "I guess I'm the green bean girl?"

I grimace. "That doesn't have the same ring to it. Maybe you should trade places with whoever's packing the sweet potatoes."

"Why, so you can start calling me sweet potato?"

I shrug innocently. "It makes a better pet name than green bean."

On the other side of Anna, Tamara groans. "Oh, for crying out loud, just put your items in the boxes and send 'em down the line." She points a finger in my direction. "Save your flirting for later."

Anna and I exchange looks, like we've been scolded by our teacher for misbehaving in class.

Further down the line from Tamara are Kelsey and Madison, who haven't stopped giggling since we arrived. I'm hoping they won't neglect to place their items in each and every box. Thankfully, Lois is standing on the other side. Someone needs to keep the girls on task.

Kurt pulls a flattened box from a pile and folds it, then finishes up with a long strip of tape on the bottom. He sets it on the conveyor and gives it a little shove in my direction. I add one container of milk, push it toward Anna who adds green beans, and then it continues down the line.

Since I began working on the design for the new distribution center, I've taken several tours of this facility. But being here as a volunteer, seeing how things run, I can get a much more accurate picture of the needs the new building will meet. Alvin Reed wasn't exaggerating. Our community really was in desperate need of a bigger warehouse to handle the storage and distribution of all this food. This current one is packed—there's barely enough room between shelves to place a conveyor, and the forklifts have trouble turning around in the tight spaces. Thankfully, the new facility is almost twice the square footage of this one.

Another box appears in front of me, and I snap to attention.

Kurt has become a box-taping machine. Unless I want to cause a backup, I'm going to have to focus—although all I really want to focus on is the person standing beside me. Unfortunately, the rattle and hum of the rollers as boxes slide across the conveyor combined with the beeping of forklifts backing up makes this room a less than ideal place to have a conversation—not to mention the fact that the ceiling is twenty-five feet high. Sound just travels upward and floats away.

About twenty minutes later, my phone buzzes in my pocket. I pull it out and see that it's Steven Hayes, the principal at South Elementary, whom I've been trying and failing to connect with for several days. I push the green phone icon on my screen, but unfortunately, this warehouse is a dead zone. I only have one bar of antenna, and I can't make out a word the man is saying.

I hold up my index finger, as if Steven can somehow see it from wherever he's calling. "Hold on a second," I say. "Let me get to a spot with better reception." I place my hand on Anna's shoulder. "Sorry, I have to take a phone call. Can you handle both the milk and the green beans for a little while?"

"Of course," she says, smiling.

"Thanks."

Kurt's brows rise as he steps toward Anna. "Just the opportunity I've been waiting for. We haven't had much of a chance to talk without this guy around," he says, hitching his thumb toward me. "I have so many stories for you."

My stomach drops.

Anna folds her arms and swings a very satisfied gaze in my direction. "Really? I would love to hear stories about Daniel. Tell me everything." She grins, and suddenly I don't feel like leaving her here with my brother-in-law.

I clear my throat and bring the phone back to my face. "Um, Steven? Can I call you back in about two hours?"

# CHAPTER 28

# *Anna*

Our small but hard-working band of volunteers packs boxes until the food bank closes at five, then we shuffle out into the cold, dark evening. It snowed while we were inside, and each of our cars is now covered in a light layer of snow. Our feet make footprints on a blank canvas of white as we cross the parking lot. It's not much—an accumulation of only half an inch, tops—but with the parking lot lights shining down, everything shimmers like it's covered in a blanket of crystals.

Clean. Beautiful.

Beside me, Tamara leads a worn-out Kelsey to their van. She presses a button on her key fob, and the rear door slides open. "I suppose we'll see you at home?" she says as Kelsey climbs in the back seat.

I nod. "I'll be home soon. I just have something to give to Daniel." I give her a knowing wink.

"Ah, yes. It's time to make the exchange."

"Now, you're sure you want to return the you-know-what?" I ask. "Because we don't have to."

Tamara shakes her head. "I feel a sense of relief, actually. I think we're doing the right thing, focusing on what really matters this Christmas. And we'll each have an extra hundred dollars in our pockets again."

"I won't complain about that." I take a step back, then offer my sister a wave. "I'll see you at home in a little while." I turn and head in the direction of Daniel's truck. The rear door of his crew cab is open, and he's helping Madison climb in. Once she's secured in her seat and the door is shut, he turns to face me.

"Hey," he says.

Just one short, three-letter word is all it takes to set my heart to thumping. "Hey," I reply. Craving just the slightest bit of contact, I place my hand on his forearm.

He looks down, then back at me, and his gaze intensifies. His Adam's apple bobs up, then down as he swallows.

I drop my hand and clear my throat. "So, um, I have the TeddyTab in my trunk. Can I give it you now? Will you be able to put it somewhere where Madison won't see it?"

"Sure," he says, rubbing a hand along the back of his neck. "She won't see a thing beneath the truck bed cover. I'll return the bear tomorrow morning before our last gift collection. Oh, and remind me to give you your money back. I still have the envelope on my desk at home."

I smile at him. "I'm in no hurry. I trust you."

I'm parked three cars away from Daniel, so I make my way to my car, careful not to slip in the parking lot—it may have been cute the first time, but I don't want to make a habit of it—and pop open my trunk. Daniel follows behind and meets me at my car, ready to relieve me of my burden. I reach into the trunk, grab a brown paper shopping bag by the handles, and hand it over to him. "Here you go."

He takes the bag. "Now we're sure about this?"

I nod. "I talked to Tamara. She's good with it. But if you still want to give it to Madison, that's totally up to you."

He shakes his head. "I really don't think she needs it anymore. I may have felt downright desperate at the beginning of this Christmas shopping season, but things have changed. Besides, I have another idea for Madison. Kurt is helping me out with it. He's actually going to pick it up tomorrow, then he'll keep it at his house until Christmas."

"Ooh, I'm intrigued," I say. "Are you going to tell me what this mystery gift is?"

He presses his lips firmly together. "Hmm ... I don't think so. It'll be a fun surprise. You can see it when you come over. I mean ... whenever that might be." He looks down at his feet and kicks at a tuft of snow.

"Are you inviting me over?" I ask. "Because I would love to come. I've been wanting to see where you live and what your life is like outside of work and volunteering."

His gaze returns to meet mine. "Well, this weekend we'll both be wrapped up in the gift program—no pun intended."

I roll my eyes. "Yes, we'll be pretty busy."

"And I'm putting in extra hours leading up to Christmas so I can take a couple days off."

"When is your first day off?"

"Christmas Eve. Would you ... want to come over then? Unless you have family commitments. I don't want to intrude on your holiday."

I shake my head. "You wouldn't be. We're celebrating on Christmas morning. If we do anything on Christmas Eve, we'll just be attending our church's candlelight service, but that's not until eight. I could do both."

His eyes light up. "Great. My parents will be at my house all day on Christmas, and so will Kurt, but Christmas Eve will be low-key, just Madison and me. I'll make dinner if you want."

"Or I can bring something too. It doesn't matter."

"So it's a date?" he says, his brows raised high.

I grin. "I hope so."

"Good." He hugs the bag to his chest and starts backing away. "I'll see you tomorrow morning. Until then, give some thought to what you'd like to do on Christmas Eve, okay?"

*Some* thought? I'll be lucky if I can think of anything *but* Christmas Eve for the rest of the night.

*Daniel*

After a thrilling supper of sloppy joes, chips, and raw carrot sticks, I dedicate the rest of my evening to working in the garage. I've got a little woodworking shop set up in one corner, and a propane heater suspended from the ceiling so I don't freeze during the winter. I really need to finish Kelsey's stable, and tonight I've recruited some help.

Madison sits in front of my workbench on a metal stool. She's wearing a bib apron and a pair of safety glasses that are way too big for her face, but she looks so cute I don't have the heart to tell her she probably doesn't need them. We won't be using any saws or sanders tonight. I have all of the wooden pieces cut out and ready to go. They just need to be assembled.

"Okay, Madison," I say, clearing off a large space for us to work. "We're making Kelsey a stable just like yours for Christmas. Do you think you can help me put the pieces together?"

She shimmies back and forth on her stool. "Yes. Can I use the drill?"

Madison loves the drill, but she has a habit of overtightening and stripping screws. "Um, maybe, but mostly we'll be using glue for this project. Your job will be to hold the pieces still while the hot glue sets. First, we need the base." I pull a rectangular piece of plywood from the bottom of my pile of precut pieces and settle it in front of us. Then I grab a bottle of wood glue from the shelf above the workbench.

"Okay, we'll start with the back wall of the stable," I say as I pick up another thin piece of wood, then turn it over. I run a thin strip of glue on the underside, leaving small gaps for hot glue, which helps the pieces stay in place while the wood glue dries. "Then we'll add a couple dabs of hot glue and ... there." I set the back piece on the base and tell Madison to hold it still for a few minutes while the hot glue dries.

We do this with all three outer walls of the stable, then the inner stall dividers and posts, and finally, the slanted roof. I stand back and brush my hands together. "Okay, what do you think so far?" I ask Madison.

"It looks just like mine!" She looks up at me with wide eyes and a smile that makes me feel like the most talented dad in the world. "But Daddy, mine is red and white. Can this one be red and white?"

"Of course it can. We'll paint it to match yours, but that will be the last step. First the glue has to dry."

After the stable's frame is up, Madison helps me attach some stall doors using the screwdriver from her little tool kit that I bought her for projects just like this, and then we make some accessories—a feed box, a fence, and some jumps. I'm only assuming that Kelsey's horses like to jump and run around as much as Madison's. Madison's horses occasionally fly *over* the stable, even though they don't have wings. They're very impressive.

I ruffle the top of Madison's head, then place my hands on her hips and lift her off the stool. "You'd better head on up to bed now. Tomorrow is another big day. We're going to meet Anna and Kelsey at Big Dealz so we can shop for some gifts. Now remember not to mention this stable to Kelsey. It's her Christmas gift, and we want it to be a surprise."

Madison runs her thumb and forefinger across her lips in a zipping motion. "I won't say a word, Daddy. I promise."

I carefully take her safety glasses off. "Good girl. Now brush your teeth, and I'll be up in a minute to tuck you in."

Before I follow her into the house, I stop and take one last look at the stable. I really hope it's something Kelsey will like. It's certainly no Teddy Tab. It has zero bells and whistles, and requires a child to use her imagination a bit more, but I think Anna, Tamara, and I all agree that that's a good thing.

These girls aren't going to stay young forever, and the time for playing with horses and dolls is going to come to an end eventually.

I take a deep breath and let it out slowly. Man, it would be nice if time could just slow down a little.

# CHAPTER 29

# *Anna*

On Saturday morning, Kelsey and I walk through the sliding glass doors at Big Dealz for our final round of donation collection, and to shop for the kids whose ornaments are still hanging on the trees. Greg and Sophie, a married couple who has been helping with donation collection, have already pulled the remaining paper ornaments from the trees in both banks. Daniel, Madison, and Kurt are stopping by the other stores on their way here. They should be here any minute. Then all we have left to do is shop for the remaining kids using the information listed on the gingerbread ornaments.

Thankfully, there aren't too many ornaments left—just a small stack, maybe fifteen, twenty total. Sophie takes the stack and splits it three ways, then hands some to me.

"Actually, I'll take a stack for Daniel, too. He'll be here soon."

"Where will I be?" his voice sounds from somewhere behind me.

I turn to see him approaching, his trademark smile lighting up his face, and his flannel shirt sleeves rolled halfway up his forearms. My heart does a little flutter—until I notice that he's here alone. I dip my head toward my niece. "Tamara's snagging a little extra sleep because she works tonight, so I brought Kelsey with me. I thought Madison was coming."

Daniel chuckles. "Don't worry. Madison is here. She's walking around the toy section with her uncle, showing him everything she thinks we should buy for the kids today." He leans close to me and cups his hand over his mouth. "I had to find a way to distract her so I could return the TeddyTab." He winks before taking a step back.

"Oh, I see." I nod my head in an exaggerated fashion. "I didn't realize you already did that."

"Yep. I didn't want it hanging over my head any longer." He reaches a hand around to his back jeans pocket and pulls out an envelope. "I also have this for you."

I take the envelope from him. It's the cash and rain check I'd left on his desk. "Thank you. I might use my half today to pay for gifts."

"You don't have to," Daniel says. "Alvin told us to request reimbursement from the Child and Family Services Department."

"I know, but I haven't made my donation yet, and I really want to pick out some gifts that are specifically from me." I hand him a small stack of paper ornaments. "What do you say we get started shopping? Once we've purchased all the gifts, we can load them into your truck along with what's in the donation box."

"Works for me." Daniel greets Greg and Sophie, and we each grab our own shopping carts. Greg and Sophie take off down the aisle. Daniel looks at me and raises his index finger. "To the toy department," he says.

I shake my head and laugh. "Remember, we also have to buy socks and clothing items for each child, not just toys. Their sizes are written on the ornaments for a reason."

He grimaces. "Maybe I'll just handle all the toys, and you can get all the clothes. Does that sound like a plan?"

I bump his legs with my cart. "No, we're going to shop one child at a time, and we're going to do it together. This will be fun."

He rolls his eyes. "I think your idea of fun is a little different than mine."

When we make it to the toy aisle a few minutes later, we run into Kurt and Madison. Madison holds up a stuffed unicorn with an iridescent rainbow-colored horn. "I picked this out for one of the kids!" she says, beaming.

Daniel takes it from her and nuzzles it against her cheek. "That was really thoughtful of you," he says to her before handing it back. "But we have to use the list on the back of these paper ornaments when choosing gifts. Why don't we look through these red ones here, and see if we can find a little girl who likes unicorns or stuffed animals."

Kurt holds out his hand, palm up. "I can do that."

Daniel waves a hand through the air. "Don't worry about it, Kurt. Thanks for your help with ... you know, earlier. You're free to go if you want."

The skin around Kurt's eyes crinkles as he appears to give the matter some thought. "Nah, I might as well help you guys with your gift-buying endeavors." He pulls half the paper ornaments from Daniel's grip, then gestures to Kelsey. "I'll take both girls with me and we'll pick out some *really* nice presents."

This feels like another attempt to get Daniel and me alone—not that I'm complaining.

"If you're sure," Daniel says. "Just remember, the toys should only cost ten to twenty dollars each. For clothes, you just get what is written on the paper."

Kurt salutes him. "Got it, Captain." He waves his hand. "Come on, girls. Don't listen to what he just said. Pick out whatever toys you want. The sky is the limit." He turns back to us and winks, then commandeers my cart, pushing it down the aisle with one little girl on either side.

I look up at Daniel and grimace. "He's just kidding, right? About the spending limit?"

He chuckles. "Yeah. Kurt talks big, but he's really a rule-follower at heart. He'll be fine."

Daniel insists on pushing our only remaining cart while I peruse the shelves. I'm currently shopping for an eight-year-old girl who likes dolls—and not baby dolls, but the kind you dress up in trendy clothes and style their hair.

"This one's in the price range," Daniel says, pulling a box from the shelf and turning it over to read the back. He hands it to me to examine.

The doll inside the box has purple skin, green hair, and vampire teeth, and she's wearing a too-short leather skirt. "Daniel, this is an *Undead Coed*. Haven't you heard of them? They're zombie dolls."

"Uh ... why would I know that?"

I roll my eyes. "I think the pale purple skin should give it away, but if not, maybe the name might be a clue."

Daniel takes the box back and returns it to the shelf, facing it backwards so the doll isn't visible. "I don't understand kids these days, or their toys. No wonder I had no idea what to buy Madison. I feel a little out of touch."

"I think that's a good thing." I sidle up beside him, my hand brushing against his as I grab the edge of the cart handle. "Let's find a different doll for this little girl. One that's actually alive."

He quirks a brow. "Anna, I hate to break it to you, but *none* of these dolls are actually alive." Then he smiles at me, and my heart threatens to leap from my chest.

Once we've selected a more appropriate doll—one that we would feel comfortable buying for Kelsey or Madison in a couple of years—Daniel holds out the next gingerbread ornament in his pile. "I think we'll have more fun with this one."

I lean over to look at the writing on the green paper. "A six-year-old boy who wants farm animals and tractors. Now that's innocent." We weave in and out of the toy aisles until we come to an aisle full of die-cast tractors and plastic farm playsets. "How about one of those semitrucks?" I say, pointing to a long box just above my eye level.

Daniel pulls a box off the shelf containing a dual-axle farm truck and horse trailer. "Here. This one looks fun. It comes with a few horses."

I smile up at him. "Great. Let's get him that one." Daniel places it in the cart and we meander down the aisle looking for more farm toys. "Do you ever wish you had a little boy?" I ask.

Daniel stops mid-stride, and I instantly regret my question. How could Daniel have any more children, boys or otherwise, if he no longer has a wife?

"I'm so sorry," I say, shaking my head. "I don't know what I was thinking. It's none of my business."

He smiles and it quells my embarrassment. "It's a fair question," he says with a shrug. "Leah and I weren't done having kids. We were thrilled to have Madison, and I would've loved for her to have a brother. Life just took us by surprise. If I ever ..." He clears his throat, then runs his hand through his hair and suddenly becomes *very* interested in a package of plastic hay bales. "That is ... *if* I were to remarry someday, I hope to have a few more kids. I never intended for Madison to be an only child."

My cheeks feel hot. I'm desperate for a way to veer this conversation back to safe, comfortable territory. I clear my throat and pick up a rubber cow so I don't have to look Daniel in the eye. "I loved having a sister. Even now, we're best friends."

Daniel resumes pushing the cart forward, keeping his gaze focused in the same direction. "Do you want kids of your own someday?"

"Of course." I dare to glance at him, then away. "Being Kelsey's favorite aunt is great, but she's not my own child. Knowing how much I love her, I can only imagine what it'd be like to be a mother."

"I hope someday you get to find out."

"I hope so too." I tug at my sleeves to remove my coat. Has

someone turned up the heat in here? The air is suddenly thick. In order to shift gears completely, I make a move I hope doesn't backfire. I toss my coat into the cart, then grab the handle and take off running down the aisle. It may come across as childish, but I'm desperate.

Daniel doesn't seem too turned off by my antics. "Does someone have aisle rage?" he calls after me. I can hear his footsteps gaining on me.

"Maybe," I call over my shoulder.

Now we're full-on racing down the aisle. I turn the corner and nearly collide with a store clerk dressed in a red shirt. I skid to a stop, then notice it's the same bald-headed clerk who gave me my rain check on Black Friday.

He eyes me and Daniel suspiciously. "Ah, you're back. Did we get the bear situation sorted out?"

Daniel straightens. "Yes, sir. All sorted out." He gives the man a thumbs-up.

"Good. I'm glad to see you ... behaving like adults." The clerk quirks a brow, then walks away.

As soon as he's out of sight, we burst out laughing. "I can't believe he remembered us," Daniel says, raking a hand through his hair.

"I can. The way we were acting, I'm sure we were pretty hard to forget."

# CHAPTER 30

# *Daniel*

A late-nineties-era sedan pulls up to the side door of the food bank. When the driver rolls his window down, I walk up to greet him. "Merry Christmas," I say. "I'm Daniel. Can I have your family number please?"

He hands me a slip of paper through the window. It has the number twenty-seven on it.

"Great. I'll get those gifts and be right out."

"Thanks," the man says as he presses a button and pops his trunk open.

After I locate all of the bags inside with the correct number on them, I bring them out and load the gifts into the man's trunk. Another volunteer, Matt, comes up beside me, wheeling a cart loaded with food. He carries the holiday meal box over to the car's trunk, nestling it right beside the gift bags I've just placed there while I grab the pie and smoked ham from the cart and place them inside. Once everything is loaded, I close the trunk, then slap it with my palm. "Have a merry Christmas." The driver of the vehicle waves at me through the back window before pulling away from the curb.

An hour or so later, Alvin Reed walks up beside me holding a clipboard. He flips several papers over the top and folds them down, revealing a paper with a list of family names and check-marks beside each of them. "Well, that looks to be the last of them," he says, indicating the red minivan that's now turning onto the road. "I'd say this was a very successful afternoon."

"I would agree." Successful and busy. It's been nonstop since I arrived here at three. That was the soonest I could slip away from the office. Some of the other volunteers, including Anna, have been here since noon. Everyone has gone above and beyond to make this day happen, and I couldn't be prouder to have been a part of it.

But I'm also really glad it's over.

As soon as I leave here, I have to pick Madison up from the sitter. Then later tonight, after she goes to bed, I plan on painting the stable we made for Kelsey. The glue is dry and the structure seems to be holding together well. I want it to be ready to go home with Anna when she comes over on Christmas Eve.

Speaking of Anna, she's walking up to me now. The lapels of her wool coat are pulled up close to her cheeks, and she's tugged a white knit hat down over her ears. She looks all bundled up and cozy, but the red splotches on her cheeks tell me she should get inside soon.

"Are you heading home?" I ask her.

"Yeah, I probably should. Tamara works at seven, which means I'm babysitting tonight." She eyes me curiously. "Do you have any exciting plans?"

"What, like a hot date?" I laugh, then shake my head. "No. I'll be spending the evening with Madison, as usual. I'm also going to work on Kelsey's gift."

Anna's eyes light up. "Oh, I can't wait to see it."

"You'll see it Friday night."

"That's right." She rubs her gloved hands together. "I'm looking forward to it."

"Me too." I'm looking forward to it and feeling insanely nervous about it at the same time. I'm planning to ask Anna to make things official, to finally stop tiptoeing around the idea of dating and just jump in with both feet. I've also been dying to kiss her, and since I don't make a habit of kissing my friends, I really want to upgrade our relationship status.

The sound of her throat clearing draws my attention upward, and I realize I've been staring at her lips. I swallow hard. "Um, yeah, so I guess I'll see you Friday?"

Anna snickers. "Yes, I'll be there at five. I'm bringing caramel brownies, so you don't need to worry about dessert."

"Great. Madison will love that." I take hold of Anna's shoulders and bring her close for a short and somewhat awkward hug, which really makes me unsure about how kissing her is going to go.

I blow out a calming breath, then take a few steps back. "Have a good night, Anna." I shove my hands into my coat pockets, then turn around and head for my truck.

Madison and I are just finishing our supper when there's a knock on the front door. "I'll get that," I say. "You eat the rest of those peas."

Madison frowns.

"Hey, they're good for you." I jog through the living room and then to the front door. When I pull the door open, I find Kurt standing on my porch holding a large cardboard box.

"I have a delivery for you all the way from the North Pole, otherwise known as Tucson, Arizona," he says.

"Ah, your parents' gifts must've arrived. Come on in," I say. "We can take them into my office." I step aside so Kurt can fit through the door with the box, and then I take it from him so he can remove his shoes.

"The delivery truck just brought this. I took what was mine, and then I headed over here without thinking about the time. Sorry if I'm interrupting supper."

"You're not. We just finished." I gesture toward the kitchen.

"Go ahead and grab a plate if you want. There's plenty of extra food."

His eyes widen. "Thanks. I ate at home, but I can always eat again."

Don't I know it. Kurt's stomach is a bottomless pit. I've never seen the man full.

While Kurt makes a beeline for the kitchen, I head into my office with the oversized box. After using the corner of the box to nudge my stapler to one side and a small stack of books to the other, I set it down on top of my desk, then sneak out of my office, shutting the door behind me.

Kurt eats two helpings of hamburger macaroni hot dish, then sets his dirty plate in the sink. "Thanks," he says. "That was great. I was starving."

Like I said—bottomless pit. I thank him for delivering the gifts, then see him out the door.

"Why was Uncle Kurt here?" Madison asks from where she's seated on the couch clicking the remote to find a cartoon.

"Uh ... he just had to bring something over. Listen, Madison, I'll be in my office for a few minutes, so why don't you pick out something short to watch, okay? Then maybe we can play a game before bed."

"What game? Memory?"

"Whatever you want, honey. I'll be right out, and then we can decide."

I return to my office and close the door. After lifting the cardboard flaps, I pull one wrapped gift after another from the box and place them beside it on my desk.

Man, my in-laws must've spent a fortune to ship this. I close one flap, eye the black-and-white shipping label, and cringe. Yep. They did. It'd almost be cheaper for them to fly the gifts home themselves. Or, they could send money and tell me what to buy. I'd be glad to do it.

But that would take all the pleasure of Christmas shopping away from Bev, who just loves finding special gifts for each person. That must be where Leah got her talent for always picking the right gift. It was in her blood. Maybe next year, I'll suggest that my mother-in-law do her shopping in September, before she and Joe go down south for the winter. Then the gifts will already be here where they need to be. No exorbitant shipping costs required.

I pull out the last festively wrapped gift and set it down, but the box still isn't empty. There's something in a white plastic shopping bag that's still taking up a great deal of space inside. I pull out the bag, set it down, and instantly my mouth goes dry. Even through the semi-transparent plastic, I recognize the packaging and the bold, red block lettering.

It's a TeddyTab.

"Oh boy." I scrape my fingers across my scalp. Leah's mom got Madison a TeddyTab. How did she even know she wanted one?

Inside the bag, I notice a piece of paper. I pull it out and unfold it. It's a note.

*Daniel,*

*Kurt told us you were having trouble finding one of these bear tablets and asked us to look down here for one. I was fortunate enough to find one in a local department store. It was the last one on the shelf, so I snatched it up. I probably should've called and asked, but that would've ruined the surprise. If for some reason Madison doesn't need one after all, I've included the receipt.*

*Have a merry Christmas,*

*Bev*

I rub my chin with my thumb and forefinger while I stare down at the bear. I still don't want to give it to Madison, even if it's not from me. Is that wrong? To deny her one of the gifts her grandparents intended for her? Am I just being a scrooge? Maybe I'm making too big an issue out of this whole TeddyTab thing. It *is* just a toy, after all.

I shake my head. No, I've already given this issue plenty of thought, and I've made up my mind. My reasons for not giving

Madison a TeddyTab are valid, and I shouldn't feel like I have to change my mind.

I'm glad Bev gave me the option to return it, but this bear came from a store we don't have here in Minnesota. So I either have to mail it back to her, or try to arrange a return online. Since both of those options require going to a post office when there are only four shipping days left before Christmas, I would have to be crazy to try and do it now. I'll deal with this *after* the holidays.

Meanwhile, I need to hide the TeddyTab. If only I'd opened the box while Kurt was still here. Then I could've sent the bear with him, just to get it out of the house. But I can't worry about that now.

I take a deep breath, then blow it out. Shaking my head, I pull the plastic bag up over the TeddyTab box, then walk over to the small closet in the corner of the room. I pull open the sliding door, shove the TeddyTab into the very back of the closet, and cover it with an old quilt. "There," I say, shutting the door. Out of sight, out of mind. At least for another week. Brushing my hands together, I turn to look at the rather large pile of gifts on my desk. Now to deal with these.

I decide to take a handful of gifts at a time, bring them into the living room, and tuck them under the tree.

Madison sees them and springs from the couch. She runs across the room, practically bursting with glee. "Presents!"

"These are from Grandma Bev and Grandpa Joe," I tell her. "And no, you can't open them until Christmas morning."

She claps and jumps up and down. "I can't wait!"

I chuckle, but I know she *can* wait, and she *will* wait, and then in no time it will all be over. After the many weeks of growing anticipation, Christmas morning comes—and then it's gone for another year.

I remember what it was like to be a child, when the waiting for Christmas morning was like a shot of adrenaline, an almost physical sensation. And year after year, without fail, what followed was disappointment. Even if I got everything on my list, everything I asked for, I couldn't help but feel let down when it was all over. That shot of happiness I got from opening gifts on Christmas morning was nothing but a short-term fix for a soul-deep yearning.

What I truly wish for my daughter is for her to know that there is only one gift that brings joy that won't fade. Only one gift can fill that need deep in her soul—in everyone's soul—and that's Jesus, the true gift of Christmas.

I may have felt like a scrooge a few moments ago, but now I'm pretty sure I'm making the right decision when it comes to Madison's presents—not only the presents she'll receive this Christmas, but also the one that was given to her over two thousand years ago.

With that particular present in mind, I walk over to the bookshelf and pull my Bible free. "Hey, Madison," I say, snagging her attention from the tree. "Can you come over here and sit for a few minutes? I want to read you a story."

# CHAPTER 31

# *Anna*

As if Daniel asking me to come over on Christmas Eve wasn't enough to send my heart rate soaring, the little "pep talk" that Tamara gives me before I leave seals the deal.

"He's going to ask you to be his girlfriend. I can feel it," she says. "Why else would he have invited you over on a holiday?"

"Because he's off work today, and tomorrow is the actual holiday. Notice how he didn't invite me over for Christmas dinner."

Tamara shakes her head. "No. You're downplaying the importance of this step in your relationship. Ten bucks says he wants to make things official." She grabs both of my arms and shakes me. "I bet he's planning to kiss you. Text me immediately if he kisses you!"

Now I'm definitely having palpitations. I'm sweating. My hands are shaking. "Maybe I should call him and tell him I'm sick."

"Absolutely not!" Tamara's practically shouting.

"Mommy, is Auntie Anna in trouble?" Kelsey asks from the other side of the living room.

I slap my forehead while Tamara winces. "No, honey," she says. "We're just having a conversation."

"You're using the same voice you use when I'm in trouble."

"Sorry, honey. I'll use my inside voice."

With a huff, I shimmy out of Tamara's grasp and turn to grab my coat off the wall hook. "All right, I'm going."

"Remember to text me."

"I will not text you."

"Okay, fine. But if you're having a really good time, don't worry about trying to make the evening service. Kelsey and I will go. You just stay with Daniel as long as you want."

So here I am, standing on Daniel's doorstep holding a pan of brownies in my trembling hands. My nerves are firing on all cylinders while I wait for him to answer my knock.

When he pulls open the door, the smile that spreads across his face holds enough wattage to light up an entire neighborhood of Christmas lights. Instantly my apprehension melts away.

"You came," he says.

I chuckle. "Were you worried I wouldn't?"

We stare at each other for a few moments. Then, as if realizing I'm still standing in the cold, he jumps back and gestures for me to come inside. "Take off your coat," he says as he takes my brownie pan from me. "I have cider and hot chocolate on the stove. I didn't know which you would prefer."

"Can I have both? One now and one later?"

"Sure." He stares at me, smiling. "I still can't believe this."

"What?"

He shrugs. "You. Here."

I narrow my gaze. "Is there something going on I'm not aware of?"

He scratches his cheek. "Maybe. I guess we'll see." He shows me where to hang my coat in his hall closet, then leads me into a room with a gas fireplace, a couch and recliner, and a colorfully decorated Christmas tree with twinkling lights. "Have a seat," he says, nodding toward the leather couch. "I'll take these brownies to the kitchen and then I'll get you some cider. I'll be right back."

Once he's gone, I settle into the couch and take a deep

breath. *Tamara may be right. Is there something special about tonight? Other than the fact that it's Christmas Eve, that is. Is he planning to ask me to be his girlfriend? To make things official?*

*I sure hope so.*

And now my nerves from earlier have returned with a vengeance.

For dinner, Daniel cooked ribs in the oven. He said they took four hours, and I don't doubt it.

"These were amazing," I say, wiping my fingers on my napkin. "I loved everything. Thank you for making dinner."

"You're welcome. Actually, Madison mashed the potatoes. She loves to help in the kitchen."

Madison ducks her head and smiles.

"Well, thank you, Madison. Dinner was wonderful."

A blush covers her cheeks. "You're welcome. Now can I have a brownie?"

"Sure you can," Daniel says. "Do you want ice cream with it?"

"Yes!" She nods excitedly. "And can I have chocolate syrup and sprinkles on top?"

"Sure. Let's go all out." Shaking his head, he turns to me. "How about you? Do you want ice cream—or anything else—with your brownie?"

I chuckle. "Actually, I'm pretty full. I think I'll wait." I turn my attention to the pot on the stove. "But I will have some hot chocolate."

He perks up. "Oh, right. I'll get that in just a minute."

I watch as Daniel retrieves a bowl from the cupboard and makes a brownie sundae for Madison. He's such an attentive and patient father. It makes me sad for Kelsey, but hopefully Tamara and I make up for it.

Daniel carries the sundae to the table and sets it before Madison. "All right, pumpkin, you need to stay at the table to eat this," he says.

Madison grabs the spoon and digs in. Within minutes, her mouth is covered in chocolate sauce, and there's a sprinkle on her nose.

I snag a couple of napkins and hand them to her.

Daniel fills two mugs with hot chocolate, then turns to me. "Should we go into the living room and sit by the fire?"

"I would love that." I get up and follow him to the living room. He places the mugs on the coffee table, then takes a seat on the couch. I lower myself onto the cushion beside him, then turn so I'm facing him.

As soon as I do, Daniel takes my free hand in his and laces our fingers together.

My heart thrums inside my chest.

"Anna," he says.

"Daniel." His name comes out as a whisper.

He clears his throat. "I have to confess I've been thinking about a lot of things lately. I've been making plans—future plans —and as crazy as it sounds, I can picture you in those plans. But I realized I never asked you what *your* plans were, short-term or long-term. Are you staying in Lake Valley? Or are you just here while your sister gets her schedule figured out? Do you have a reason to go back to Seattle, like a job, or ..." He swallows. "Or anything else?"

I squeeze his hand. "No, I don't have anything waiting for me there. I think my future is here in Lake Valley."

His warm brown eyes sparkle in the firelight. "I'm glad to hear that." He leans in close. "Anna, I really like you." Reaching a hand up to my face, he runs his thumb across my cheek. "I'm so glad you're here."

I lick my suddenly dry lips. "I'm ... very glad to be here."

The hand that was on my cheek slides around to cup the back of my neck. Daniel pulls me closer. I respond by leaning forward until my forehead is so close to his, I can feel the energy pass between us. It's like a live wire, or one of those Fourth of July sparklers that kids wave around. You can feel the sparks, but they don't hurt.

If either one of us moves a fraction of an inch, our lips would touch. But since Daniel has the most at stake here, I'm letting him take the lead.

"Anna, is it okay if I … I mean, I would really like to—"

The door to the kitchen bursts open. "Daddy, we have to show Anna the stable!"

As Madison runs right up to the couch, a bucket of disappointment dumps over my head, dousing me like a campfire, its flames snuffed out, charred logs left smoking.

Daniel jerks back, then looks between her and me.

I squeeze his shoulder. "It's okay, Daniel. I'm not going anywhere."

A spark flashes in his eyes. "Madison's going to bed early tonight," he mumbles as he rises to his feet.

I press a hand to my lips to smother my laughter.

Daniel motions toward the hallway. "I'm going to put a few finishing touches on Kelsey's gift, and then I'll bring it out to show you. I want it to be perfect before you see it." He turns to Madison. "While I'm in the garage, why don't you show Anna the ornaments you made for the tree this year? I'm sure she'll be impressed with your artistic talent." He casts a knowing look over his shoulder and then disappears down the hall.

"Okay, Daddy." Madison walks over to the tree and pulls down two ornaments, then hurries over and holds them out to me. One is a snowflake made from craft sticks and sequins, and the other is a glass bulb with a snowman on it made out of white-painted thumbprints—Madison's, I assume from the size of them.

I take the glass one from her for a closer look. "Wow," I say, turning it over in my hand. "This is beautiful. They both are. Your dad wasn't exaggerating—you do have talent." I hand the ornament back to her. I start to shiver, and look down to see that I have goosebumps on my arms. I glance to the left and notice that the gas fireplace has shut off. It must be on a timer. "It's a little chilly in here," I say to Madison while rubbing my arms.

"It usually is," she says. "My daddy is always warm, and if I tell him I'm cold, he says to get a blanket." She perks up. "I know where I can get one for you."

"Thank you," I say. "I would love that."

Madison disappears down the dark hallway, and when she comes back she's holding a blue-and-white quilt. No sooner does she hand it to me than she takes off down the hallway again. This time she's gone for several minutes. When she finally returns, her eyes are as big as two jelly donuts, and in her hands is something I thought I'd seen the last of.

A TeddyTab.

# CHAPTER 32

# *Anna*

I swallow hard as I stare at the little girl in front of me who is clearly thrilled to be holding a TeddyTab.

"Look what my Daddy bought for me," she says, holding the bear out in front of her.

For a moment, I'm speechless, trying to wrap my head around what I'm seeing. "Your … daddy?" I repeat.

Madison shrugs. "I think so. I didn't ask Santa for a TeddyTab. I asked him for something else. And Santa leaves his presents under the tree, not in the closet, so it has to be from Daddy, and it has to be for me because who else would it be for?"

Who else indeed?

My stomach churns as I watch Madison dancing around with the bear in her hands. I'm certain that Daniel said he returned the TeddyTab. He told me *to my face* on Saturday morning, before we went shopping, that he'd just come from the customer service desk. Was he lying? I didn't actually see him return anything, so I can't know for sure.

Or maybe he returned it because he didn't need it anymore, because he'd already found *another* one for Madison, one that he got for an even lower price. But why wouldn't he tell me?

*Because you made a big deal about not wanting to give one to Kelsey.*

Could that be it? Did he not want to tell me he still wanted to give Madison a TeddyTab because I didn't think it was the right gift for Kelsey? Surely he'd feel comfortable talking to me about it —unless ... unless maybe we don't know each other as well as I thought. Maybe he doesn't trust me.

Maybe I shouldn't trust him.

I catch Madison's eye and motion toward the bear with my index finger. "You should put that back where you found it," I tell her. I hold out the quilt to her. "And put this back too. If your dad did buy this for you, he probably wanted it to be a surprise."

She takes the blanket from me and runs back down the hall. When she returns a few moments later, she's empty-handed. "I put it all away."

"Good." I rub my hands up and down my arms, then stand.

At that moment, Daniel returns from the garage with a big smile on his face. "It's all ready for you to come take a look."

I press my lips together and glance down at Madison, then back up at Daniel. I release the breath I'd been holding. "You know what? I think maybe I should get going."

Daniel furrows his brow. "What? It's not even eight o'clock."

I shake my head rapidly. "I know. I just ... I think I made a mistake skipping the candlelight service at church. I should be there with Tamara and Kelsey." I make my way toward the hall closet, then open the sliding door and search for my coat. "Thank you so much for dinner. It was all very good."

Daniel places his hand on my shoulder. "Anna, what is going on?"

Tears pool in my eyes. I turn my head away as I slip my arms through my coat's sleeves. "Nothing. I'm fine, really. I just think I need to be somewhere else right now."

"But the stable. You'll take it home with you, right?"

I stop and think for a moment. Kelsey has no other big gift if not for the stable. Depending on what happens with Daniel, I can always pay him for his time and materials. I can't deny Kelsey this gift, though. "Um, sure. Do you have a box you can put it in? I want to protect it as best I can. I'll meet you outside."

Without looking at Daniel, I slip my shoes on and turn toward the front door. "Goodnight Madison. I hope you have a wonderful Christmas tomorrow with your grandma and grandpa."

She says goodbye, and I head out into the cold, snowy darkness. While I'm digging through my purse for my key fob, Daniel comes out of the house carrying a large box. I find the fob, click the trunk button, and wait for Daniel to load the box into the back of my car. He firmly shuts the trunk, then walks around the car to meet me where I'm standing beside my open door.

"Please tell me what happened in there," he says, hitching his thumb toward the house. "I know something changed while I was gone. I can't make it better if you don't talk to me about it."

He's right. I should talk to him about it, and I will—but not tonight. I don't want to ruin his Christmas with his daughter. He should be able to give Madison whatever it is he wants to give her without feelings of guilt attached to it. But that doesn't mean that he and I should be together. I can't be with a man who isn't upfront and honest with me. I don't want someone who does things behind my back or who withholds information from me. Maybe I'm damaged, but that's just how it is. I've learned my lesson, and I won't make the same mistake twice.

I fold my hand over the top of my car door and look up into Daniel's eyes. "I want you to have a wonderful Christmas with Madison and your parents. Enjoy being with them. I'll talk to you in a few days, all right?"

His jaw clenches, and I watch as his Adam's apple bobs up and down. "Are we not okay anymore?" He waves a hand between us. "Whatever this is, it's not finished. Not for me."

I swipe a finger beneath my eye, where a single tear has managed to escape. "We'll talk soon. I promise." I get one last glimpse of him through blurry eyes before lowering myself into my car seat and shutting the door. I start my car, and, without warming up the engine as much as I should, I back out of the driveway and pull away.

Realizing I can make the church service just a few minutes late, I head straight there from Daniel's house. I park in the first open spot I find, then dash across the snowy parking lot toward the front door. I slip into the darkened sanctuary just as the congregation is rising to sing the first carol.

I spot Tamara and Kelsey four rows up from the back, standing right at the end of the pew. I hurry up the aisle and slide in beside Tamara. When I gently knock her hip with mine, she scoots over the slightest bit, then turns to me with wide eyes. "Why are you here?" she whisper-shouts. "I thought you would still be at Daniel's."

I shake my head. "I left. I'll tell you later."

We sing three more carols, and all the while I can feel Tamara's gaze on me. I refuse to look back at her, for fear I'll start crying. I force my lips to stop quivering and form the familiar words of the beloved choruses. To distract myself from thoughts of Daniel, I peer around the sanctuary. Hanging from the walls on both sides of the large, open space are quilted banners in gold, blue, red, and green, displaying words like *Savior* and *Messiah*. *Prince of Peace* and *Emmanuel*.

God with us.

Reminded once again of the true meaning of Christmas, I close my eyes and pray.

*Dear Jesus,*

*Forgive me for losing sight of you with the many distractions of this season. I pray that you would be with all of those who are hurting or hungry this Christmas. Bring them comfort. Let them know you're there with them. I thank you for the many blessings you've given to me and my family. We don't take them for granted.*

*I want to ask for clarity in my relationships, especially one in partic-ular. I don't want to hurt Daniel, but I also don't want to be hurt. I just want to know the truth before I lose my heart to him.*

*Amen*

I open my eyes and sigh, knowing full well that I may have already lost my heart to Daniel. I can only pray that he gives it back in one piece.

# CHAPTER 33

# Daniel

The rest of Christmas Eve crawls by slower than Madison's pink motorized SUV with a drained battery. I tuck Madison in for the night, kiss her on the forehead, then send one final text to Anna before going to bed myself. It goes unanswered, just like the two before it.

Lying in bed and staring at the ceiling, I try to run through the events of the evening, searching for any clues as to what I may have done wrong. Did I say something? Was the almost-kiss too much too soon for her? I can't think of anything else it could have been. It was almost as if a switch had been flipped. Things were going so well between Anna and me, and then ... they weren't.

Without any answers to my questions, falling asleep is challenging. I toss and turn, and finally doze off sometime after checking my phone at two a.m.

On Christmas morning, I wake up groggy, having gotten almost no sleep. My parents arrive shortly after breakfast, and Kurt shows up just minutes later. I make an effort to smile throughout the gift exchange, not that it's *that* hard. I'm truly thankful that my parents are with me and Madison, but my mind is somewhere else. I need to talk to Anna. She told me to wait a few days, and I will, but the waiting won't be easy.

We save the gifts from my in-laws for last, and once Madison and I have opened those, it's time for the big reveal—Madison's gift from me. Or … Santa. I'm not sure who it's from, but since I can't exactly slap a gift tag on it, it doesn't really matter. All that matters is that Madison likes it. Or *him*, to be exact. I'm hoping I read all of her cues correctly, the not-so-subtle hints that she'd drop whenever we were shopping or talking about gifts. If I didn't, well, I guess it's too late now anyway.

I nod to Kurt, and he stands up and walks toward the door to the garage. Meanwhile, I crawl over to Madison and wrap an arm around her shoulder, pulling her close to me. "Did you have a good Christmas, sweetie?"

She nods. "Yes. Did you? Did you get everything you asked for?"

*Not exactly.* "Uh … yes, I did. It's been a good day so far." I turn to see my mom and dad looking on expectantly. Everyone knows what's coming. Everyone but Madison, that is. I give her shoulder a squeeze. "I'm really glad you've had a good day so far, but I think there's one more present waiting for you in the garage. Would you like to see what it is?"

She hops up onto her feet and gives me an open-mouthed smile that reveals all her little teeth.

"Okay, I'll take that as a yes." I stand and take her hand, then lead her down the hall toward the garage door. Then I nod to Kurt, who opens the door. Within seconds, an untamed ball of golden energy comes bounding over the threshold and into the kitchen. It slides across the linoleum, makes a U-turn, then jumps up at Madison, practically knocking her down before licking her face all over with its long, pink tongue.

"Daddy!" she squeals. "It's a puppy!"

I can't contain my sigh of relief. She *did* want one. Thank goodness. I'm not sure what we would've done if she didn't—we're kind of committed either way. "This is your puppy, Madison," I say. "Do you know what you want to name him?"

She turns to me, the dog still licking her cheeks. "We should name him Licky!"

I wrinkle my nose. "Or, we could think about it for a while and then circle back."

Chaos ensues for the next hour or so as the dog tears through the entire house until finally wearing himself out and curling up in my mom's lap for a snooze. I didn't know any gift could possibly cause more trouble than a TeddyTab, but so far, this one's coming in at a very close second.

Finally feeling like I can relax, I bring a warm mug of coffee to my lips and take a sip, then swallow. I cradle the mug in my hands and lean back against the couch. I turn to Madison, who's sitting in front of me on the floor, playing with some new toys. "Wow, that was an action-packed Christmas morning, wasn't it Madison?" I say, nudging her in the side with my toe. "Can you say thank you to Grandma and Grandpa for the nice gifts and then we'll start making lunch?"

She turns to my parents and says, "Thank you."

"You've very welcome, sweetheart," my mother says as my dad ruffles Madison's brown curls.

Madison turns her gaze back to me with a puzzled look and wrinkled brow.

I lean forward, resting my elbows on my thighs. "Is something wrong, honey?"

"Did you forget about the TeddyTab?"

I jerk my head back. "I'm sorry, what did you say?"

She holds her hands out to her sides. "The TeddyTab. Did you forget to wrap it and put it under the tree?"

I'm pretty good at interpreting Madison's little-girl speak, but this time I'm stumped. "I don't know what you mean. You asked Santa for a puppy. You said so earlier. Are you sad that you didn't get a TeddyTab?" I take another sip of coffee, hoping the caffeine will lend me some mental clarity.

She shakes her head. "I'm talking about the TeddyTab from *you*, Daddy. I found it. You hid it in your office, and I found it when I was looking for a blanket for Anna. You can ask her. I showed it to her."

I choke on my coffee. "You what?" Wiping my chin with the back of my hand, I scoot forward, closer to Madison.

"You left her alone, and she said she was cold, so I went to get a blanket. There was a TeddyTab under the blanket! I showed it to Anna, but I don't think she liked it very much."

My heart lurches. "This was last night? And you didn't tell me?"

"You were in the garage." She splays her hands like, *Dad, keep up with the story.* "Then Anna said I should put it away, so I did. I put it back in the closet."

I slap my palm against my forehead and groan. I'd been way too careless.

"It's still there," she says. "I'll go get it." She rises to her feet.

"Wait—" I reach out my hand, trying to snag Madison's sleeve.

She turns back around and gives me that same wrinkled-brow look of confusion.

"Madison, honey, that present was ... well, it wasn't from me. It was from Grandma Bev." And now that Madison has seen it, am I supposed to tell her she can't have it? I sigh. This is a mess. I wave my hand, beckoning her back to me. "Honey, Grandma Bev sent the TeddyTab just in case you wanted one, because they were hard to find here in Lake Valley. But I didn't give it to you because it's very expensive, and it's probably a better toy for older kids."

Saying nothing, she nods.

"If you want, we can save it for a few years until you're ready for the responsibility, but I'd rather give grandma's money back to her. In a few years when you're ready for your own smart tablet, you might not want one that's attached to a teddy bear. But by then, it will be too late to return this TeddyTab to the store."

She looks thoughtfully up at me. "Then we should do it soon."

I raise my brow. "You're okay with that? You're not sad about the TeddyTab? Uncle Kurt thought you might want one." I eye my brother-in-law, and he shrugs.

Madison tilts her head. "I maybe do want a TeddyTab, but I want a puppy more. That's why I asked Santa for one. I told you he knew what I wanted."

Yes, she did, and I'm not sure how I feel about "Santa" getting all the credit for bringing Madison the right gift this year. I'm pretty sure that between now and next Christmas, we're gonna have to have "the talk" and put an end to the jolly bearded man's involvement in our Christmas celebration, but we won't do it today.

I take Madison's hand. "Honey, Kelsey also wanted a Teddy-Tab, and her mom and Anna decided not to get her one, either. So when Anna saw that you had one that she thought was from me, I think she got a little upset. That's why she left in such a hurry."

Madison's eyes get wide. "Then what should we do?"

"I think we need to pay them a visit and explain what happened," I say. "And if that's not enough, we are going to do whatever it takes to make this better."

# CHAPTER 34

# *Anna*

Kelsey has brought every last plastic horse from her bedroom into the living room, where she's lining them up in front of her new stable. Which she *loves*. Daniel had the perfect idea for a Christmas gift for my niece, and after seeing it, my heart is one big mess of thankfulness and regret and love and mistrust and doubt and desire—and I don't know where to go from here.

"Look, guys," Kelsey says to her horses. "This is your new home." She leans back on her heels and smiles, then picks up a horse and settles it into one of the stalls.

Tamara leans close to me on the couch where we're sitting, watching Kelsey play. "There's a lot of love built into that stable, and I'm pretty sure it isn't all directed toward Kelsey."

A wave of shame washes through me. "I know."

The stable is beautiful. It's the most beautiful Christmas present I've ever seen. Daniel put so much time and effort into every little detail. He hand painted the board-and-batten siding, adding bushes of colorful flowers along the side and back walls. There's a little ladder leaning up against one side that he made out of tiny pieces of wood. He even cut out a few little squares of plaid wool to make saddle blankets for the horses. He thought of everything.

And it makes my heart hurt.

Tamara shakes her head at me. "Stop being stubborn and text him back. He's sent you, what, three messages? And you've ignored them all."

"I don't know if I can trust him. He lied about the TeddyTab."

"Maybe he did, but maybe he didn't. You haven't even asked him about it." She wraps an arm around my shoulder. "At least give him a chance to explain. I don't want you to lose this man over a misunderstanding—or your stubborn pride. You're going to have to be vulnerable. Yes, you could get hurt, but for the last time, he's not Wayne. He's also not your ex-fiancé who doesn't even deserve to be taking up so much real estate in your mind! Forget about him. Go to Daniel's house. Talk to him."

I scratch the side of my face. "Do you really think I should? What if he's mad at me?"

Tamara shakes her head at me, then pushes hard against my back. "Go."

"Okay, fine. No need to get bossy." I stand and run over to the door, then realize I'm wearing sweatpants and a T-shirt with a Santa cat on it that says "Meow-y Christmas." I grimace. "I should change first."

"Stop wasting time!"

"Okay, okay. I'm leaving." I pull my coat from the hook on the wall, slip my feet into my boots, then turn the knob and open the door. There on my front porch, staring back at me with the most heartbreakingly gorgeous brown eyes I will ever see in my life, is Daniel. And right beside him is Madison.

"Hi," he says.

I lift my jaw up from the floor, then say, "Hi."

"Can we talk?"

My heart reverberates against the walls of my chest. "Um, sure." I take a step back to let them in. While they take off their boots, I push the door shut tight. "Madison, Kelsey is introducing her horses to their new stable. You can play with her if you want."

She clasps her hands together, then runs over to the tree and slides in right beside Kelsey, who hands her a horse to play with.

Tamara hops up off the couch and feigns an exaggerated yawn. "Wow, I'm feeling tired all of a sudden. I think I'm gonna catch a nap. Otherwise, I might not make it through my shift tonight."

I roll my eyes. She's never been a good actress, but I love her to death.

Daniel follows her with his eyes until she disappears down the hall, then he turns his attention to me. "Can we sit?" He gestures to the table. "There's something I need to explain."

We each pull out chairs from the kitchen table. Daniel sits facing me, his knees practically touching mine. "That TeddyTab, the one Madison showed you last night, was from her grandma. Leah's mom. I had no idea she was sending it. I didn't ask her for it, but apparently Kurt mentioned that we were having trouble finding another one, so she mailed it. I got it Monday and didn't have time to deal with it, so I shoved it in the closet and put it out of my mind. To me, it didn't even matter. I wasn't aware that Madison showed it to you until this morning. I came here as soon as I found out. I'm so sorry for the misunderstanding."

I stare at him for a while, at the concern etched into his brow, the way his eyes are glistening, the stubble on his jaw revealing that he didn't shave this morning, and I am suddenly aware of how wrong I was. How careless I was with his heart. Again.

"I'm the one who should be sorry," I say. "I jumped to conclusions. I should've asked and saved us both a lot of trouble."

He reaches for my hands and takes both of them in his. "I don't want this to come between us. Last night, I had planned to tell you that ... I don't want to be just friends. I want to be more. A lot more."

"You owe me ten bucks," a muffled voice says from a short distance away.

My jaw drops. I swing my head to the left and right, but the source of the voice is nowhere in sight. "Tamara, I thought you were taking a nap," I say, my words floating up into the air, not finding their target.

Daniel snickers, then pulls my hands up to his lips, kissing the knuckles on one hand and then the other. "What do you think?"

To be honest I'm having trouble thinking about anything right now. I take a breath and hold it a moment before exhaling, allowing some time for my infatuation-induced brain haze to clear. Then I lean forward and place a kiss on his lips—just a peck. "I think I'm really glad you're here. And I think I want to see where this goes. You and me."

He hesitates for only a second before leaning in and capturing my mouth with his. Sweet and slow, it's a kiss that erases my doubts and opens my heart to a future—an exciting future—with Daniel. And Madison.

I wrap my arms around his neck and tug him closer and then—

A loud whisper. "They're kissing." Then giggles. Lots of giggles.

I pull away, feeling my face flush. "I think they've seen enough for now."

Daniel looks down at our knees touching. He laughs and shakes his head. "Like I said, I have no idea how to do this now that I have a little girl."

"It's okay," I say, cupping his chin with my hand and lifting his head until our eyes lock. "We'll figure it out. We have plenty of time."

# CHAPTER 35

# Anna

APRIL

The harsh spring wind tosses my hair and ruffles my skirt. Daniel wraps an arm around me and pulls me close. To my left, I notice Alvin Reed making his way across the lawn toward us. He's dressed in a brown tweed suit and a tie—but the most noticeable addition to his wardrobe is the scratched-up, gray hard hat on top of his head.

"Looking good there, Mr. Reed," Daniel says. "Aren't we supposed to wait until the photo op to put those on?" He gestures to the top of Alvin's head.

"The rest of you do, but I don't live by the same set of rules." He chuckles. "The shovels and hard hats are lined up and ready to go."

I look beyond Alvin's large frame to the future site of the new distribution center, where a bulldozer is parked, and in front of it, a large trench has been dug. The dirt from that trench is piled up in a long row, and in that pile of dirt are eight long-handled shovels with hard hats covering their handles, ready and waiting for those who will be involved in the ground-breaking ceremony.

Alvin hikes a thumb over his shoulder. "The photographer from the paper is here, so we'd better make our way up there."

Daniel turns to me and grips my shoulder with his free hand. "I guess I should go. The ceremony starts in a few minutes."

"Of course," I say. "I'll be watching from here." As he pulls away, I grab his hand and yank him back toward me. "I'm so proud of all the work you've done here. This is going to be a wonderful facility."

He presses a hand to my cheek. "Thank you, Anna." Stepping closer, he gives me a quick kiss. "I'll be right back." He taps the tip of my nose with his index finger.

Footsteps approach beside me. "You've got yourself a good man, there."

Surprised, I turn at the familiar voice. "Tamara, you came! I thought you were at work."

She waves a hand through the air. "I wouldn't miss this. I mean, who doesn't love a good ground-breaking ceremony on a freezing cold April day?" She hugs her arms to her chest, then rubs her hands up and down her biceps.

"Why does it seem like all the most pivotal moments in my relationship with Daniel involve standing outside in the cold?"

"Because it's been winter the entire time you've been dating. But don't worry, the worst is over. Soon the sun will come out and stay out. Hopefully. And just think—you'll finally get to see what Daniel looks like in shorts. Have you ever even seen his legs?"

I punch her lightly in the arm. "Yes, and they're perfect."

"Of course they are." She makes a gagging face. "Hey, just so you know, I can't stay long. I snuck out during my lunch break."

Thankfully, Tamara managed to snag the day shift at the clinic, and her new schedule has made life so much better for her and Kelsey. She's home in the morning before school, and her shift ends only an hour after Kelsey's school day. And she never works weekends anymore.

"No matter how long you stay, I know it'll mean a lot to Daniel," I tell her.

"Speaking of Daniel, I brought an invitation for him and

Madison to come to Kelsey's birthday party next week. Can you make sure he gets it?" She reaches into her coat pocket and pulls out an envelope.

"Of course." I take it from her and slip it under my arm. "I'm sure Madison will be thrilled to come. Can I invite Kurt, too? He loves cake, and, as you know, he's usually available."

Tamara snickers. "Sure, he can come. Does he know how to make balloon animals by any chance? We need some form of entertainment, and I'm hoping to hire it on the cheap."

"I doubt it, but I'll ask. You never know, he could have many hidden talents none of us are aware of."

Tamara raises a brow. "I doubt that."

"Oh, and in case Daniel asks, what does Kelsey want for her birthday?"

"Hmm." Tamara purses her lips. "You know, I did hear that the TeddyTab 2 is coming out soon. This time, it's not only a mini-tablet with built-in GPS, but it's also got a camera and a phone."

I throw my head back and groan. "Please tell me you're kidding."

Tamara's sly smile gives her away. "Do you honestly think I'd want to go through all that again?" She shakes her head. "Tell Daniel to get Kelsey a tub of ice cream and a spoon. She'll be ecstatic."

I can't help but laugh. "I won't do that, but I will tell him not to make a big deal over her gift."

"Thanks. She already has everything she needs."

And it's true, she does. Although Kelsey's relationship with her father could be better, she did get to see Wayne on Easter. He made it back to Lake Valley for an extended weekend and spent part of Good Friday and almost all of Easter Sunday with Kelsey. Now that he's officially moved to North Dakota, I don't expect that we'll see too much of him, but things are moving in a positive direction. He's been texting and calling more, and he continues to send money every couple of months, so that's something.

A crackling noise pulls my attention to the ground-breaking site, where Alvin Reed has just stepped up to a podium mic—much like he did on the night of the auction back in November—and the irony is not lost on me. It's almost a full-circle moment. And how strange that this big, boisterous man would've played a small but significant part in my and Daniel's love story.

But God works in mysterious ways, as I've well learned over the past few months.

A hush falls over the crowd that has gathered.

"Thank you all for coming. I'm Alvin Reed, executive director of the Northern Minnesota Food Bank's board of directors. On behalf of the area food banks, the City of Lake Valley, and the Department of Child and Family Services, I'm proud to welcome you to the future site of the first distribution center to serve our tri-county area. It has been an honor for me to work alongside so many of you as we endeavor to meet the needs of those in our community who find themselves without enough to feed their families."

As Alvin continues to talk about all of the ways that the community has pulled together to make this day a reality—the fundraising, the design, the forthcoming construction—it reminds me of all the little details of my life that I can't see, and yet they all manage to fall together perfectly in God's timing. He's always working behind the scenes, and I don't need to worry about my future. My life is safe in his capable hands.

I'll be forever thankful that God led me back to Lake Valley, and that somehow, Daniel and I found our way to each other in an icy parking lot on a cold November morning. It's crazy to think that we both went there in search of a toy that neither of us ended up keeping, and we left with something that neither of us knew we needed—each other.

We definitely got more than we bargained for.